THE LINGERING
DARK

KINGDOM OF STARS BOOK ONE

JADE CHURCH

THE LINGERING DARK BY JADE CHURCH FIRST PUBLISHED IN GREAT BRITAIN BY JADE CHURCH IN 2022

HARDBACK ISBN 978-1-7398968-6-7

PAPERBACK ISBN 978-1-7398968-5-0

EBOOK ISBN 978-1-7398968-4-3

INTERIOR ARTWORK BY WARICKAART AND ALICE MARIA POWER

COVER ARTWORK BY NIRU.SKY

ALSO BY JADE CHURCH

Temper the Flame

This Never Happened

Get Even (Sun City #1)

In Too Deep (Living in Cincy #1)

Coming soon:

Fall Hard (Sun City #2)

Tempt My Heart (Living in Cincy #2)

CONTENT WARNING

The Lingering Dark contains themes and content that some readers may find triggering, this includes but is not limited to: *blood, gore, death, violence, mentions of disease and war, death of a parent, manipulation/abuse by a parent, alcohol, panic attacks.* Please note, this book also contains on-page sex, swearing, and nudity.

CONTENTS

NAME GUIDE

SAIPH - SAY-IFF

AUREN - OR-REN

ORIEN - OR-REE-EN

VALENTINA - VAL-EN-TEE-NA

FALLON - FAL-EN

MYRRIN - MIR-IN

TAZLEN - TAZ-LEN

RAZE - RAY-ZZ

KARA - CAR-AH

VALA - VAH-LAH

HENNICK - HEH-NIK

GLOSSARY

ELORIA - THE CAPITAL OF VIRIDIS WHERE SAIPH MEETS ORIEN AND VALENTINA

SOMNIA - CAPITAL OF SOMMER WHERE VALENTINA FIRST MET ORIEN

CAMBER - DESTROYED TOWN THAT SAIPH FIRST WALKS THROUGH WHEN SHE ARRIVES

ASTOR - ANOTHER DESTROYED TOWN IN SOMMER

SOMNIUM - THE TREASONOUS NAME OF THE WHOLE KINGDOM

VIRIDIS - THE NORTH

SOMMER - THE SOUTH

QUAESITUM - CONQUER

AETHERES PROCIDENS - FALLING SKIES

VICTORIS - CONQUEROR

VICTOR VICTIS - CONQUEROR TO THE VANQUISHED

BALTEUS - BELT

VINDEX - AVENGER

IUDICIUM - JUSTICE

IUDI - JUDGE

VIDI - I SAW

STELLULA - LITTLE STAR

ANIMA LUX - SOUL LIGHT

IGNIS CORDIS MEI - FIRE OF MY HEART

IGNIS - FLAME/FIRE

SEREN - SILVER

THE LINGERING
DARK

PROLOGUE
ONE HUNDRED YEARS PREVIOUS

SOMETHING FOUL IS COMING, THE MAIDS WHISPERED AS they fluffed pillows and sent gusts of wind out from their hands to beat down the deep orange draperies. *There is a chill in the air—There is death on the breeze—I heard the Forest moan.* It was the last that captured the attention of Agatha, nursemaid to the heir apparent. Whispers from the Forest were never something to be taken lightly but, of course, that all depended on the generation. For the young maids, the Forest was eerie, yes, but it was difficult to fear something that seemed innocuous when they all knew there were greater, more powerful monsters lurking among the stars. But Agatha remembered the stories of old Gods and magicks, the last imprints of which were said to reside within the depths of the Forest that curled around the edges of their world and slept at the foot of the estate's boundaries.

"What did you hear?" Agatha asked primly,

standing from the rocking chair in the corner of the room and placing the babe down into a crib where she began to kick and coo. The maids ceased their hand waving. The mop stood still in mid-air and a few stray feathers floated softly to the ground as they looked between themselves as if deciding who would be taking this fresh blow. At last, one of the younger maids stepped forward, tilting her chin demurely so a strand of frizzy red hair spilled from her lace cap to brush the top of her cheek.

"It-it says only one thing, Madame."

"Spit it out, child," Agatha said sharply, chin wobbling from the force of her mouth.

"*Run.*"

The maids broke down into nervous titters and the youngest girl's cheeks flooded red as Agatha regarded her silently. No, the infrequent murmurs of the Forest were not to be taken lightly at all. But the imaginations of a young maid, eager to prove her worth…

"That's quite enough of that. Out. Now."

The maids didn't wait to be told twice and fled the room in a swirling of skirts and cotton. The fine wrinkles in her hands creased more deeply as Agatha squeezed them together. Should she report these mutterings? It was more than likely that these were merely the fancies of a young maid, hoping to gain some notice. But if they were not… if there had indeed been whispers…

A loud *boom* seemed to shake the castle, jolting Agatha from her thoughts. Nonsense, likely nothing more. Light flashed from behind the drapery as a quiet rain descended and Agatha realised for the first time that the room had grown dark, the lightning brightening the interior and then plunging them into darkness once more. A lingering smell of smoke had Agatha turning automatically toward the large candelabra's place on the table at the side of the room. Moving easily in the grey-dark, she could see the flames had likely been extinguished on a stray breeze as the storm rolled in. The room was too big for the babe, drafty and empty, somehow foreboding as the sound of thunder filled the air, intertwining with the steady cry that was echoing from the crib.

"I think this will be a loud one, my sweet. Would you like to see?" Shushing gently, Agatha scooped the child into her arms and swayed closer to the large bay windows which looked over the stone courtyard. There, overseeing the estate like a guardian, was the very Forest the maid had mentioned. The trees were so large that it was said the tops could reach the stars themselves, though nobody dared climb them to find out. Things had been... better since the marriage of the king and queen, but venturing into the Kingdom of Stars would still be a journey for either fools or those with a death wish.

The trees seemed agitated, swaying unusually in the heavy wind that groaned throughout the estate, and Agatha shivered, tucking the babe's blanket more tightly around them. Normally the Forest brought Agatha a strange sense of comfort, though she possessed no magick of her own. It was said only those with the gifts could hear the words from the old Gods that lurked within, but the longer Agatha looked out of the window the more she thought the trees might be screaming. The clouds churned black and the pine needles seemed to ripple, making the hairs on Agatha's arms stand straight.

The babe burbled softly as it peered past Agatha and gave a jolt as a wave of light flashed across its face.

"Now, now, it was just a little lightning," Agatha murmured, but despite her words, she could not look away from the Forest. As if it were willing her to *see* to *hear*. Then all at once, the sky fell true black. It was not the black of night or the heaviness of a storm—it was the complete absence of starlight, a darkness that it was said could cause madness if one was left within it too long. Agatha's breath choked in her throat as the skin across her body tightened, pebbling in air that suddenly felt heavy as she frantically tried to swallow. Gasps of relief tore from her when the sky lightened a moment later, but her heartbeat did not settle. Neither did the trees.

It had seemed a long time since Agatha had seen or felt that darkness. She could have lived without ever feeling it again. A soft wail made Agatha's arms close instinctively tighter around the babe as another bright slash of silver rippled through the air. "We must go."

For it had not been lighting she had seen flashing in the darkness, but a sword, a word, glowing so brightly it would forever be seared into her eyes. *Quaesitum.*

Agatha knew who bore that blade. If they were here, then the time had come to run. *Aetheres procidens.*

The window before them burst in a tinkling of sound that made the babe scream as Agatha spun, shielding them with her back to the sky and holding her long cloth sleeve to the babe's face where a sliver of glass had struck.

Her feet moved quickly to the cupboard and the bag already packed and then to the door to do her duty. To leave her king. Her queen. Her home.

All she could do was buy them fragments of time and hope it would be enough.

The thick carpet runners covering the stone floors quietened her steps as she moved toward the rope at the end of the corridor, to the emergency bell, pulling so hard it burned her hands as she tugged and tugged until a blast of sound sent her ears to near shattering.

Glass had spilled from the window next to the bell, crunching beneath her feet, letting in the night air. Too late, she had been too late. She spun away to the other rooms to ensure the safety of her kingdom's hope.

Agatha's feet pounded the halls, her skirts billowing out and tangling around her steps, but she could not afford to slow. It was to her detriment, as her legs slid out from under her in her haste, and her mouth went dry as she skidded along the stone floor and used her own body to once more shelter the child. She tried to rise quickly, knew there wasn't a moment to waste, but her feet caught on the heavy material of another skirt as she fell, clutching the babe desperately to her chest.

It was the auburn-haired maid. Red poured from her throat as she scrabbled frantically, as if trying to hold the garish wound closed, and bile rose in Agatha's throat. Blood coated Agatha's side and slicked through her hair where her body had fallen across the maid's, but she could spare no time to wipe it away, nor to end or aid the young girl. She was already dead, and Agatha had to keep moving. Before all was lost.

She rounded the corner of the next corridor hurriedly. Her heavy skirts made her fumble constantly, and her bonnet had been lost some time ago. A shrill wail split the night, and Agatha froze for a second before picking up her bloodied skirts in her one free hand and running, trying her best not to jostle the babe tucked into her arm as she went. She flew through the familiar open doorway of her second charge and stilled as she saw the heavy oak door, carved with depictions of stars and moons, on the floor. Hinges intact.

Her eyes slowly lifted, and a breath left her mouth in a relieved sigh as her eyes met the king's. All was not lost. The king was alive, and none on the mortal plane were so powerful as he. Agatha did not yet know what had become of the queen. She could only hope that the mother of her charges and fair ruler of Somnium would also live to see the dawn.

Time seemed to slow and gutter as a spill of blood slowly trickled from the king's mouth, his blue eyes burning so brightly she felt them sear her soul. The brilliant blue shifted slightly towards the crib at her back, kept separate from its twin in the hope that should an intruder find one heir, they might not find the other before meeting their swift end. The king's mouth moved in one final command that told Agatha all she needed to know about who had come for them this night: *Run.*

She nodded slightly, eyes wet as the king slowly began to fall towards the ground, revealing the dark-haired woman standing behind him, eyes burning amber and sword still wet with blood.

The king heaved his final breath and screamed, white hot magic shooting through his veins and lighting him up as brilliantly as the sky at dawn, and the woman shouted in dismay as it scorched outward. The tapestries became ash, and the draperies seemed to drift away with the breeze. The light shot out of the windows and lit up the sky, pouring outwards defiantly, as if to signal to anyone watching, waiting, that after the dark, there was always light. The magic flowed around Agatha as gently as a breeze, the king shielding her and his children even in death, as the king of the mortal plane did the last he could with his dying magic —*nova.*

Agatha took her chance and seized the other babe from the crib, ensured both were tucked safely in her arms, then bolted. A shout of rage followed her, but the wave of light from the king's released powers burned impossibly brighter, protecting her back as Agatha made her way to the only safe place left.

Run.

CHAPTER ONE
SAIPH

"If you think she doesn't know what you're doing up here, you're a fool."

Saiph startled from her seat at the window. Though she was in one of the tallest towers of the castle, she wasn't looking out at the view it gave over the city, her kingdom. Rather, she'd been using the power she'd recently acquired to peer through the veil that separated her plane from that of the mortals'. It was a power accessible only by the queen and her heir, as only they were able to channel enough considerable power to do so, and Saiph had been abusing it for several weeks since her mother had named her as such and shown her how to wield it.

Saiph peered wryly at her twin as she let go of the magick she'd been using. The location she'd chosen didn't matter much for piercing the veil, but it helped her to focus without the distraction of the other stars—it also had the added benefit of being practically abandoned. She wasn't really sure why they had such a large castle when the majority of it went unused.

"I'm sure that I don't know what you mean," Saiph said as she stood in one fluid motion. "I'm just... clearing my mind." Her peace disturbed, Saiph made to leave the tower. Vala blocked her way, moving so quickly and silently that even Saiph was caught off guard.

"I have a message from Mother."

Now that *was* surprising—especially that she'd chosen Vala to deliver it. One of her many tests, undoubtedly.

"She has decided that you are to go to the mortal plane."

Saiph's eyes widened slightly, the only sign she would let herself give to betray her shock. Going to the mortal plane was unheard of. Nobody had walked there since... Well, since the mortals had slain the King of Stars, Myrrin.

"Why?" A strange mixture of excitement and fear curled within her—to see the mortals up close would be... Saiph clamped the thought down. She should have no interest in the mortals or their strange way of life. Their betrayal of the stars had been over a hundred years ago but, for a star, this was barely any time at all. The mortals were animals, savages, undeveloped and undisciplined, a fact her mother reminded them of during every training session they had.

"There is a mortal. A rebel. She claims she is the rightful heir to the thrones."

Saiph swept her eyes over Vala's face, trying to gauge her sister's reaction to this information. "Throne*s*? How would a mortal be the heir to *my* throne? It doesn't—"

"There are only whispers. Nobody knows who or where she is. But she is thought to be the lost child of Myrrin and Tazlen."

"Not possible," Saiph breathed and Vala nodded, her face perfectly blank.

"Regardless, the queen won't tolerate it."

"She wants me to kill her," Saiph guessed, and Vala nodded.

"Yes, and any who follow her. Mother has tried searching for them through the veil but has been unlucky thus far."

"It seems like a waste of time to me." Saiph rolled her shoulders out, stretched her arms up and let out a long sigh. She'd been sitting in that window ledge for longer than she'd meant to. If some mortal woman wanted to take the throne, she would need to go through Saiph's mother first—the thought was laughable.

Vala stepped closer and said quietly, "I do not think it is a coincidence that she is choosing to send you now, after naming you heir."

Saiph tensed. "A test." Her mother was so fond of them. Testing their loyalty, their love, their strength, their obedience, their power... This test, whether the queen meant it or not, could be an escape. Not forever, just... to breathe, even if she was surrounded by her enemies.

After the mortals had slain King Myrrin and Queen Tazlen, all talks of peace had been abandoned and Saiph's mother now ruled both planes with an iron fist, a grip that extended to her children. For once, it would be nice to leave behind this world, to do something that nobody had been given permission for as long as Saiph could remember—to walk among the mortals.

But to send Saiph now, when the timelines were about to diverge and leave the Kingdom of Stars out of sync, was telling. Her mother wanted to make sure Saiph was loyal, and what better way to do so than send her off to kill her enemies, unsupervised?

Vala saw the understanding break across Saiph's face, and she nodded once before reaching out and taking Saiph's pale hand into her own dark palm.

"You must not fail."

Saiph understood what Vala wasn't saying. She could not fail, lest it mean her own ruin and probably her death.

"I will not."

Vala stepped back, melting with the shadows easily. "You are to leave immediately."

Saiph nodded and felt rather than saw her sister leave, a quiet blessing on her breath before the room fell empty once more.

Until your light touches the sky.

It was an old saying, one hardly ever uttered now. It was frequented in the war when soldiers and spies would go to the mortal plane in a shower of starlight that streaked across the mortals' sky. It was a promise of hope but, coming from Vala now, it was clear that her sister thought Saiph was going to battle... and she was worried that her twin was right.

SAIPH HATED THE MORTAL PLANE. She hated the smell of pig shit and unwashed bodies—Mother had been right. The mortals *were* like animals. Scrabbling about in the dirt and dust that just about passed for a village, make-do homes cobbled together from sheets and twine. She hadn't realised just how much she would miss home, miss the spiralling towers of light that made up the Kingdom of Stars, and the presence of her sister. In these miserable excuses for villages there was no warmth other than her starfire, and even those she had used sparingly because of the energy drain that accompanied them. Other than the girl she'd found on her first night on the mortal plane, she'd only encountered two rebels—both young, both had refused to talk in deference of their supposed queen and heir. Both had paid with their lives. Tonight, Saiph camped in a clearing in the forest, far away from the stench of human civilisation, or what passed for it.

They had stared as she'd made her way through

the groups of campfires, some watchful, some in awe, but most were openly hostile, spitting on the ground where she had walked as if she had tainted it with her steps. The children were dirty and scrawny, small hands clutching empty bellies and mouths propped open in silent 'O's as she walked by. There were no animals. Saiph hadn't seen so much as a stray. It was hardly surprising though—what would a human know of keeping a pet? It was a wonder they didn't eat their young. There was no beauty in this ugly world, save the night sky.

It had been too long since one of her kind had walked amongst the humans and it showed. Muttered oaths, quickened breaths, and hands sneaking to hidden blades greeted her in every encampment. It was fine. She was here for one purpose alone: to hunt, as her Mother bade her. Perhaps if she'd bothered to use a glamour then she may have remained unnoticed a while longer, but she wanted them to know—this false heir and her followers. Saiph was coming for them, and the longer they hid, the more frustrated she grew.

Nevertheless, the mortals' reactions made the decision to sleep beneath the stars an easy one. Nobody would dare harm her while she slept. Not unless they valued their insides... *inside*. Saiph let a pleased smile curl her lips at the thought and watched a nearby butcher sway alarmingly at the sight. The smell of old blood clung to him, mixing not unpleasantly with the sharp tang of his fear, and she tasted it lightly on her tongue before moving past and along the outskirts of the dark forest.

Odd that the humans should band together in the open instead of taking respite under the towering firs, though there was something *off* about the mass of trees, some presence she couldn't put her finger on. But if the mortals insisted on staying out in the open, who was she to disagree? Saiph enjoyed solitude—the presence of her twin sister notwithstanding.

Against the darkness of the night, her skin glowed and she let out a sigh as she found an even piece of cold earth, lay back, and gazed into the star-strewn sky. She missed Vala terribly. This was the longest she had ever gone without seeing her twin sister. Where Saiph was lightness personified, Vala was dark. Her hair and her skin were the most beautiful ebony, and Saiph missed the soothing darkness she exuded. The only spot of brightness in Vala's face was her eyes—a warm tawny amber that occasionally seemed to just float in the air when Vala blended with the night. Saiph wondered if Vala missed her yet. Time moved differently between the mortal plane and the Kingdom of Stars, a fact they were careful to keep from the humans—if they knew there were times that even the stars couldn't watch them, well, Saiph was sure that was information that could prove fatal. To her kingdom and the humans both. They were approaching a large divergence in the timeline now. It was part of the reason her mother had chosen now for

Saiph to hunt the heir, to keep an eye on things when the stars couldn't.

A rustling sounded in the bushes to her left, and Saiph sat bolt upright. There weren't many creatures who would risk her flames and, against this darkness, it was obvious to all but the most ignorant what she was. A small fox emerged and froze at the sight of her on the ground, probably wary after so many of its brethren had been hunted by the mortals. But she was no mere mortal.

Some animals Saiph didn't mind. The fox, for one, was a clever little animal and Saiph found she enjoyed their cunning nature. She held out her hand to the orange creature and it placed a singular paw towards her, as if it could sense there was something different about her and wasn't sure whether to run. She was so focused on the fox she didn't notice the dark figure scurrying behind her until it was too late. The fox turned tail, and a blow struck Saiph in the shoulder as she turned at the last second to protect her head. Nasty little creatures, mortals.

CHAPTER TWO
SAIPH

SHE AWOKE TO THE EARTH TREMBLING ABOVE HER HEAD and could smell the dampness of the dirt, the harshness of despair as it coated the air with a thick tang, almost masking the smell of heat and blood. Mortals. She was trapped here with mortals.

Dirt rained down, dropping onto her head, into her eyelashes, and the ceiling shook as if it would crumble around them at any second. They seemed to be in some sort of smugglers tunnel deep beneath the earth. Her tongue felt thick in her mouth and Saiph's legs refused to cooperate when she ordered them to stand, to charge, to run. Her woozy mind remembered nothing, only the fox, then the pain. Dizzy as she was, she couldn't even conjure up the usual panic that being so far away from the stars would awaken. Beneath the earth she was weakened, not by much—but in a fight even the slightest disadvantage could mean death.

A small hand suddenly seized her attention as it

squeezed her own. She managed to roll her aching eyes in the direction of the young woman whose hand she now held. The woman's big brown eyes were crinkled in concern as she gazed at Saiph. With a pang, Saiph realised the woman reminded her of Vala, exuding some sort of peacefulness Saiph only usually felt around her twin.

"I'm sorry," the young woman whispered in a surprisingly proper peasant's tongue. "They spotted you in the field as they were carrying me away. You must have put up a fight, else they wouldn't have drugged you." Drugged, so much made sense now. She was grateful, in a sense, as it kept the panic that came with being underground at bay. Of the fight she remembered nothing, but was glad she hadn't made it easy for them. Whoever *they* were.

Her hands fumbled blindly at her back, searching for the dual swords she kept strapped there, and she let out a sigh of relief when she found them intact. They were hidden by a powerful glamour at all times, visible only to those who also had powerful magicks or when Saiph wielded them. Whoever it was that had taken her, they likely had no more magic than a tickle of ember under their flesh, else they would have seized her swords immediately. Star-spun steel was very valuable on the mortal plane. It lasted thrice as long as anything the mortals could churn out and was impervious to all but the strongest magickal attacks. How her kidnappers didn't know just what they had in their midst, Saiph couldn't fathom. If they did, they would likely already have dumped her somewhere, murmuring supplications to the stars while they did so. Unless the mortals had grown so arrogant as to believe they could truly best and kill a star.

The woman, however, had followed the movement of Saiph's fumbling hands keenly, dark eyes gleaming in the near-dark. Saiph couldn't see the woman's mouth, just her white teeth as they shone against the dark with a feral delight. "I hope you know how to use those," was all she said. No word about who, or rather *what*, Saiph must be in order to carry such blades and keep them glamoured. She held the young woman's eyes in the darkness before inclining her head just slightly. What Saiph really wanted to know was why they had been taken. The woman seemed to read this need for knowledge on Saiph's face, though she wasn't sure how she was able to see her so well in the semi-darkness. Magick. It had to be.

"I don't know where they're taking us. I only know that there have been whispers, magick users disappearing. Wherever we're going, people don't come back."

It was all Saiph needed to hear. The earth still trembled slightly above their heads as though dozens of feet pounded the ground, but it had eased in the past few minutes, and something deep in her soul raged about being confined beneath the surface. *Good.* It meant the drugs were beginning to wear off. Soon, she would be able to shake off the grogginess completely.

"I'm going to help you," the girl said slowly. "I wouldn't make it ten feet by myself, but together we have a fighting chance." She waited for Saiph's nod of agreement before continuing. "I can burn through the drug in your system, not completely, but I can lessen its effects, for a time. The rest is up to you. Be quick." Saiph nodded again, the drug still keeping her tongue numb.

The young woman pressed her delicate hands, marred by several broken nails, to Saiph's chest. It was clear that the woman must have fought their kidnappers hard too. Saiph wondered if they had gotten lucky, clearly catching the both of them unawares. It was likely that they would have otherwise met swift ends, judging by the power Saiph knew she could wield and what she now sensed leaking from the other woman. Odd then, that she felt she couldn't escape without Saiph's help. Perhaps she had been injured. A burn of warmth grew from beneath the woman's hands, sending a jolt into Saiph's body and chasing away some of the drug's grogginess.

The guard, a large and hairy mortal man, had noticed Saiph's sudden movement and called to someone behind him at the corner of the dimly lit tunnel. "Hey! *She's* up and moving!"

The harsh sound of his voice was abruptly cut-off as Saiph brushed her sword against his throat, moving quicker than a whisper of wind. Another man flew around the corner of the dirt path and pinwheeled his arms in the air in an effort to slow himself. It did him little good and her sword smoothly sank into his gut, knuckle deep, causing a rush of blood to cascade over her knuckles as she spilled his innards to the ground between them. For a second, he looked at them on the floor with astonishment and then his gaze clouded over in death.

A meaty fist came from nowhere, flying out of the darkness to connect with Saiph's face. With her light colouring and silvery hair, she was a beacon in the darkness that allowed the mortal to have a distinct advantage—he could see her, but she could not fully see him with the drug still lingering in her system and dulling her senses. Saiph hesitated briefly before making the split-second decision. The woman already knew, or at least highly suspected, what Saiph was, so she ripped away the small glamour she'd been using to keep her glow to a minimum with half a thought and allowed her otherworldly starlight to fill the cramped space, illuminating the sweating, thick man in front of her. It felt odd to be free of the small glamour. It was the kind she used daily at home, and now on the mortal plane too. The full force of any star's glow was blinding—some mortals had even caught aflame from being caught in its power, so the stars were taught from a young age to keep it muted. Weakened as she was, the man merely winced, but her light did what she needed. She could see.

Saiph spat blood that faintly glowed onto the floor. "That punch," she said, advancing slowly, "wasn't very nice of you."

The man's face had turned pale, his skin sallow, but a wave of dizziness made Saiph stumble, and he saw his chance. *Starlight take me!* The woman's effect on the drug was wearing out fast. She needed to end this now. The man took advantage of her dizziness and thrust his hand into her face in a clashing blow that rattled her teeth, swept his heavy foot into her stomach once, twice, thrice. Made to do so again before the young woman, forgotten on the side lines as she freed her binds, leapt onto his back with a yowl of fury. Saiph watched blearily through the blood in her eyes. The woman was like a hellcat, burning with hot flames. If Saiph didn't know better, she would have thought the woman had come from the heavens, just like Saiph. The woman's hands glowed molten red as she pressed them to the sensitive flesh of the man's face. He let out a frantic scream as his skin began to sizzle and pop. Scrambling frantically away, he tripped on Saiph's crumpled form. Her barely raised sword slid cleanly through his back as he fell, a gasp of surprise his only reaction. Using the last of her strength, Saiph shoved her sword home, showering herself in his still-warm blood.

The witch, as Saiph now realised she was, pushed the man from Saiph's body with a grunt of effort and then bent to retrieve Saiph's sword before she could murmur a warning. A warning, it seemed, the witch did not need. Her hands of flame did not so much as falter on the hilt, curiouser and curiouser, this woman. It told Saiph more than the woman perhaps realised.

The blood of the stars did indeed run through her veins. Only someone of starlight could touch her swords and live. While most mortal magick users were born with only the mortal ability to wield the elements, it was possible for starlight to breed true. But the Kingdom of Stars had long ago banned such couplings. It was interesting, therefore, that some remnant of that magick remained within mortal bloodlines so many years later.

"We must hurry, before anyone else arrives." With that, the young woman hooked an arm under Saiph's back and tugged her upwards, stumbling only a little as she pulled her towards the corner the men had rounded. There was a steep hill, and dirt rained down on their heads as they stumbled along. The young witch set her jaw and continued to drag Saiph, and she wondered absently why the mortal woman did not just leave her there to die. Burn her to ash, like Saiph had done to the rebel girl only a few nights before. The sight of that determined jaw was the last thing Saiph saw before her eyes rolled, and her body at last gave into the pain of her wounds, the crackle of flames echoing in her ears as the young witch burned that place to the ground behind them.

CHAPTER THREE
SAIPH

METAL CLANKED AS SHE STIRRED. SAIPH'S EYES fluttered open, surprised to find herself intact and that the mortal woman had not, in fact, dumped her somewhere. She tried to sit up and was pulled short by the oddly coloured chain that held her to the bed.

Perhaps she was not yet unscathed after all.

She tugged on the chains with a growl, slumping back when they refused to give—that in itself was surprising. There were not many materials that could withstand the strength of a full-blooded star. Let alone the heir to the throne.

The room was dark, and Saiph could smell dust. Normally the lack of light wouldn't have been an issue for her, so she had to assume that the foul drug still lingered in her system. The stars had many advantages over the mortals, sharper senses being only one of them, and it felt odd to feel so stunted. She couldn't hear beyond her room, couldn't taste the subtle emotional charges in the air on her tongue. Saiph felt practically... mortal. Three days she'd been on the mortal plane, *three*, and already she'd wound up kidnapped twice. Vala would have died laughing if she could see Saiph right now, and her mother... Well, it was often best not to think about Queen Fallon and what she would think of her daughter's failure.

The thing that felt the most disconcerting was that Saiph could no longer feel the sky, the thin barrier between her world and that of the mortals. She had heard that all the mortals knew of the Kingdom of Stars was the balls of ether strong enough to penetrate the veil and hint at what lay beyond. She couldn't have imagined just how breathtaking that view would be, however. The vestiges of her kingdom, scattered amongst the mortals' sky like jewels, shimmering brightly.

To be so cut-off now... it was a physical ache, a gnawing hunger, and a flash of firelight at the entrance to the room illuminated what Saiph had begun to suspect—the earth had swallowed her once more.

Panic took her, dulled still by the drug that lingered in her system, and she wondered lightly what they might have used for it to affect her so strongly. For a moment, she felt pity for those other mortals the witch had mentioned who had found themselves at the hands of Saiph's captors. The drug pulled her under again, echoes of memory calling to her oddly, and her eyes rolled back just as the firelight grew closer.

. . .

"THERE IS nobody else I would trust in my place more than you, daughter." The queen's thin lips curled into a bloodred smile that did little to warm Saiph's insides. The swords Saiph never took off seemed to tingle at her back as if in warning, though she could not imagine what would warrant such a reaction. The queen did not wish her harm. In fact, she wished Saiph to be her successor. Nothing could grant her more protection. "Unlike some of us," the queen did not look at Vala, but Saiph held her breath nonetheless, "you put the good of the kingdom first, always. You are unquestioning. Loyal. You are everything I envisioned and more, Saiph."

It was not often that Vala openly defied their mother, but it was only when she was displeased with one of them that the queen praised the other. They had been given a task, seemingly meaningless aside from the fact that their queen demanded it. To refuse was death. To assist one another was death. And when Saiph had faltered, her foot scrambling for purchase half-way up the mountain side, Vala had reached out her hand. It was a defiance their mother would not tolerate, even if it had spelled Saiph's demise. It had cost Vala dearly—the price of the throne, in fact.

It was not unusual within the Kingdom of Stars, where twins were common, for the two to reign as one—so long as it was with the previous monarch's blessing. Saiph had once hoped for exactly this but now, with Vala failing this test of loyalty, it would never come to fruition.

"You will be my sole heir, made to rule with a firm hand. Do you accept?"

"I do," Saiph murmured, keeping her eyes directed at the floor as was expected when in the presence of her mother. Vala could be her advisor when she took the throne, Saiph reassured herself. Their mother was hardly discreet when she made her displeasure known, and their people would never accept Vala on the throne knowing that it was without their beloved queen's blessing.

"You will forsake all others in favour of the kingdom. Do you swear?"

Saiph hesitated as the swords against her back warmed once more.

"Do you swear?"

"Yes, my queen. I swear."

Her mother curled a finger under Saiph's chin and smiled when she looked up before sweeping away with not a word said to Vala, whom she had essentially renounced.

"Sister, I—"

Vala stepped forward out of the darkness that had concealed all but her eyes. "You owe me nothing, sister. I am pleased for you."

"Vala…"

"I mean it."

Saiph nodded and turned away but paused as her twin called her name.

"But Saiph—be careful."

She hesitated, not knowing what the warning referred to, before nodding once and walking swiftly away.

THERE WAS a man staring at her. Saiph jerked upright, or tried to, forgetting in her groggy state about the chain that bound her to what looked like a smaller version of the beds they had in the Kingdom of Stars. The wrought metal frame bowed but did not give under her strength. She looked to the man who had watched her ministrations with a cool smirk and frosty blue eyes as she snarled. "How?"

His smirk grew. "My sister's gifts are very... adaptable."

Sister? The witch with the star blood?

"I'm Orien. You'll be staying with us for a little while." His cool blue eyes were like chips of ice as they analysed her from head to bloody toe. "You were in rough shape," he said when he noticed her looking curiously at the bindings around her ribs. "You have my sister to thank for that, as well as your life too, I suppose." Orien leaned in. His breath was as cold as the rest of him as it ruffled her silver hair. "I wouldn't have been so generous. We know what you are. The Gods know you've killed enough of us."

"Yes, well, luckily that was not your decision to make, brother," came a voice from the doorway. The lamplight cast an orange glow about the small room and bathed the slight figure in the doorway with gold. It was her. The witch.

The male rolled his eyes, the tightness of his jaw turning to granite at her presence. "This is the worst of your plans yet, dear sister. One I vetoed, remember?"

"I already told you, Ren, there's something

different about her. I can see it in her eyes. I can feel it beneath my skin. Besides, your wishes do not supersede that of our queen—take it up with her if you must."

Saiph's eyes were glued to the burning ember of a woman who slowly approached the bed where she lay. Their words flowed past her, barely of note. She could feel it too. There was something *other* about the witch, an inexplicable draw that Saiph couldn't make sense of. She had not forgotten the way the witch had lifted Saiph's sword with ease, nor the way her hands had glowed with power. The magicks mortals conjured were typically nature-based, of the elements. But there was something different about the flames the witch had conjured, like they'd burned a little too hot or a little too bright. Saiph couldn't help but wonder how much starlight flowed in this witch's veins. The brother, Ren, moved to block the witch's path, muttering to her in a voice so low and fast even Saiph could not detect it.

Who is she? Saiph wondered as the witch pushed past her brother with a mere wave of her hand, eyes taking in Saiph's form, still chained taut to the bed. The witch strode closer, ignoring the brother's dogged footsteps, brushing past him once more like he were no more than a cobweb as she grew closer to Saiph's side.

Orien's eyes locked onto Saiph, eyeing her muscles for any twitch of threat and the curl of her hands as if she would summon her fire right then and there, though she was much too drained for that right now. At least *he* hadn't dismissed her as a threat... but the witch, powerful as she was, Saiph did not think that she was a match for the power of a star.

Finally, Saiph was able to see the face of the woman she had only stolen glimpses of up until that point. Deep chocolate curls ran wild over her shoulders, flowing down to her waist, and eyes that were an odd golden amber, not the dark brown Saiph had initially thought, watched Saiph keenly. It was her mouth that truly fascinated Saiph though, hard and soft, and full but cutting all at once, a true work of art. Expressive, and marred by a scar that was pale against the soft brown of her skin, slicing through her lip and adding the edge this woman needed on the outside to show what was truly within. Dangerous. Beautiful. Tempting.

It was then that Saiph noticed what the witch was walking on. Barefoot. Dirt. Saiph's heartbeat began to thunder. Her mouth filled with saliva, and the fangs she hardly ever called upon smoothly slid down as she began to pull on her bindings in earnest.

Orien instantly had a hold of the witch. "Fangs! What more proof do you need that she's a devil?"

The witch shrugged him off once more and pressed a cool hand to Saiph's cheek while she thrashed. "What ails you?"

As if her touch compelled her, Saiph moaned. "I'm underground. *I'm underground!* Let me out. *Let me out.*" Saiph's eyes rolled as she roared the last words, frantically searching the room for escape. Bland clay walls were all that met her sight, a large woven rug thrown in the middle of the floor… and then the witch. Her eyes were bright, soothing. Suddenly they felt as deep as the night, blanketing her in their depths. Without even realising it, Saiph's breathing slowed to match the witch's, the darkness in her eyes lulling something deep inside Saiph to sleep.

"That's it, *seren*. You are not trapped. The sky is but a whisper away."

Saiph stared at her, no longer as sure of her own power against that of this woman who could command the elusive darkness as easily as breathing. "Who *are* you?"

The witch smiled, displaying white, even teeth, and Saiph discreetly peered at her canines and thought they seemed a little sharp for a mortal. The starlight had indeed bred true—this woman, this *witch*, could bend the night to her will like none Saiph had seen, save Vala.

"You may call me Auren. I'm the personal guard to the queen."

Mind settled, at least for the moment, her instincts kicked in. Regardless of the woman, the male was clearly eager for Saiph's demise. She had to get out of here, but as she looked over the pair, she feared that may not be as easy as she would have liked. Gone was the peasant's dress Saiph had felt against her in the smuggler's tunnels. Instead, Auren and Orien were clad in sturdy leather, trimmed with buckles that gleamed an odd golden colour. Saiph looked over her chains and noted the same sheen.

"You are able to charm the metal with your flames?" Saiph asked.

Auren followed Saiph's gaze to her chains and nodded, a small smile playing about her lips. "Yes. Sorry about the chains, but we had to take precautions. You're the bad guy, you see." Auren laughed at whatever expression Saiph was wearing. "You already met my brother Orien, but I wonder if you have figured out where exactly you are?"

Auren looked amused. It seemed that she had heard of Saiph, but Saiph had not heard of her. Still, Saiph was a star. She had starfire and strength and magick at her disposal. Now that the drugs had mostly faded, she was not helpless.

She closed her eyes and listened past the heartbeats in the room with her to the outside. The unfamiliar clanging of cutlery on plates, breathing and laughter, a couple rutting several doors down, the hushed conversations—"Did you hear? They've captured a *star.*"

She opened her eyes and found Auren watching her hungrily, as if she too wanted to experience the gifts Saiph had. Saiph couldn't believe her luck. She let a feline grin stretch her mouth and winced slightly as it pulled at her still-healing split lip. "I've been looking for you."

Orien shot Auren a tense look, his jaw clenched and his mouth like granite. There were some similarities between them, the shape of their mouths and eyes, but much like Saiph and Vala, where Auren was heat, Orien was frost. Their differences were palpable, and Saiph stretched out her senses, testing them. Orien could have passed for any old human, nothing remarkable, save the ice that was slowly crawling down his dark fingertips. A rare gift, but not a treasure, not like Auren. Auren's soul tasted like... starlight. Like breath in Saiph's lungs. There was something intrinsically *different* about her. Like called to like, and something in Auren resonated within Saiph. It worried her.

The witch smiled, as if she knew precisely what Saiph had done and had sensed as a result. "Yes, well, fate has a way of bringing people together. You found us. Welcome to her majesty's court."

"I don't see how a false heir can have a court."

"I wouldn't let the queen hear you say that," Orien said with a smirk. "She's been known to have a temper."

Auren rolled her eyes. "You have us at a disadvantage. You know our names, but what should we call you?"

"You may call me Highness, and you should do so on your knees." Saiph let an echo of Orien's earlier smirk touch her lips.

Sure enough, he gave a low growl, but Auren simply placed her hand on his forearm with an amused light in her eyes. "Come now, must we be so formal? We did kill together, you and I. Is that not the sort of thing to be honoured in your culture?"

It wasn't, and she was somehow sure that Auren

knew that. The tilt to her head and the smile curving those plush lips all screamed amusement. Somehow she knew enough about the Kingdom of Stars to make jokes at their expense. It was knowledge no mortal usually had access to. Did they have a spy? Saiph didn't see how that would be possible when only two people could peer through the veil, and travel between the planes was strictly monitored and not exactly inconspicuous.

The Kingdom of Stars prided itself on decorum, wanting to separate itself from their mortal subjects, whom they considered little more than savages. For all that they said though, even Saiph could admit that the Kingdom of Stars was, in her opinion, a brutally beautiful people. She had grown up with a sword in each hand and the ability to burn down the world if she had so chosen. That, to her, was more than mere savagery—it was domination, it was art.

Auren grinned as she seemed to read Saiph's thoughts from her eyes. Kingdom hold her, maybe she could even take the thoughts straight from her mind, given her previous displays of power.

"You may call me Saiph."

"Say-iff…" Orien drew her name out annoyingly, and she wanted to claw the words back out of his throat and off his tongue.

"We," she said to Orien, "did *not* kill together. You can stick to Highness." With a savage grin and the promise of violence simmering in her eyes, she was unsurprised when Orien fingered an empty loophole, evidence of where a blade would usually hang. No doubt they hadn't trusted her to be around one. Though, her chains were proving surprisingly resilient against her enhanced strength.

"See," Auren said with a tinkling laugh that instantly drew Saiph's eyes back to her, "I told you there was something different about her."

Mentally shaking herself as her eyes drifted back to the empty loophole on Orien's belt, Saiph snarled. "Where are my swords?"

Auren pointed to the wall where they were propped up. The blood had been cleaned from them, and they gleamed like moonlight once more. If she could just snap these restraints, she could reach them in one large step, maybe two. Fools. Or perhaps they felt they had nothing to worry about, but she had yet to find a set of chains that could hold her. Starlight hold her, she'd had enough practice while she trained in the dark for a year, then been held underground for two. *It's for your own good,* her mother had told her, *those mortal savages will do far worse if they ever get a hold of you.* So Saiph had trained. Trained with swords, to be both torturer and tortured, trained in magick. The only thing Saiph had never mastered was the earth. Whenever she would inevitably lose control, Vala had been there to soothe her with darkness, bless her with night skies.

"You either think very little of me or very highly of yourselves to have them so close."

Orien smirked. "Last time I checked, *you* were the one chained to the bed… *Highness.*" He spat her title like it was a curse and, despite herself, Saiph wanted to laugh at this dramatic, overprotective mortal. He had the fire of a star within him, if not their cool imperiousness. Saiph was sure Orien would be offended to hear it and smiled tauntingly at the thought.

"I'm afraid you won't be getting out of those chains unless I permit it. They are infused with my own brand of magic, mixed with gold. It creates a certain... resistance to star magick. It even holds up against star-spun steel."

"If that is true, then what is it you want with me? I have been trained to resist torture, so as much as your lapdog may want, beating me will get you nowhere."

Orien rolled his eyes and muttered an oath, but Auren just smiled that same gentle smile again.

"Why would we beat you when I only just fixed you up, hm? No. I want to propose a deal."

Saiph raised her pale brows haughtily, ignoring the flakes of blood that fell away at the movement.

Auren continued. "You owe me a blood-debt."

Saiph was surprised by the words but determined not to let it show. Who *was* this mortal-but-not woman? How did she know so much about the Kingdom of Stars? A blood-debt was to be fulfilled above anything else. To invoke one awoke old magick, the kind that even the stars had no power over. If Saiph were to refuse, any manner of price could be exacted of her by the magicks in order to cover the cost owed. Auren had caught Saiph in a bind, and she knew it, judging by the smirk she didn't quite let form and the gleam in those deep, burning eyes.

"What are to be the terms?"

"The magick users in my queen's kingdom are disappearing. I want you to help me hunt down whoever is responsible for the kidnappings. Me and mine are off-limits throughout."

"And once I find them?"

"Well, then comes the fun part." Auren practically purred the words, and a shiver of delight swept through Saiph.

"You do not belong here with them," Saiph said, nodding her head to the doorway and the sounds of human lives spilling from that direction. "You are like me. Other."

Auren gave a secretive smile. "Do we have a deal, *seren?*"

Seren, silver. Saiph let the first real smile since she'd arrived on the mortal plane grace her lips. "It is agreed. I will hunt with you, until the cost is fulfilled."

"Until the cost is fulfilled," Auren echoed, but the strange smile and light in her eyes lingered. Orien looked between the two of them, and it was clear from his tight jaw and the way his eyes kept flickering back to Saiph's smile that he was sure this was a bad idea. Like prey, waiting for the trap to spring. Saiph grinned wider and watched Orien pale. Auren let out a low laugh, and Saiph's eyes sprung back to her.

"Best not forget to seal the bargain, now, must we?" Auren prowled forward, her petite frame radiating power, and Orien ran a hand over his shaved head in agitation as Auren came close enough to touch. Saiph had wondered how well Auren knew the rules—it appeared very well. If she had failed to seal the bargain, the cost would have rebounded upon the invoker tenfold. Saiph wasn't sure whether to be delighted or disappointed. She settled for cautious as Auren moved closer.

"It is sealed," Auren murmured before pressing her mouth to Saiph's, her tongue flicking around one fang in a totally unnecessary but thrilling display of dominance. Saiph hadn't even noticed she hadn't retracted them. It was no wonder Orien had looked so disturbed by her smile—yet Auren hadn't hesitated for a second. Like calls to like, and Saiph couldn't help wondering what it was about Auren that called to her.

"Come," Auren said as she leaned away. "We have work to do."

With those words, Saiph's chains slid free as if they were live snakes, wriggling away from her wrists and releasing her from the bed. She was caught in a deal that, until fulfilled, meant the bearer and their chosen was protected. The death of the false heir and her rebels would have to wait, for now.

CHAPTER FOUR
SAIPH

"I SHOULD IMAGINE YOU'D QUITE LIKE TO BATHE," Auren said as Saiph slid her blades home in the sheaths between her shoulders. "As becoming as you look in all that blood, I think you might frighten the court."

Saiph let out a rasping chuckle that she abruptly choked off. She could not let her guard down around these people. Blood debt or no, they were her enemies and, eventually, they would die at her sword. She had finally located the rebel's base, the 'queen's court'—though there had yet to be any sign of the supposed heir herself. Saiph suspected they would keep the heir far away from the likes of her. Being able to identify the 'queen' would paint a target on her back, and that the court would likely not abide.

Maybe… she could keep Auren, for a time. Purely on official business, of course. How could it be that a mortal could contain some of the power of the stars so log after such couplings had been outlawed? Until

43

Saiph knew more about this, she should keep her enemies close, and what her mother would never know couldn't hurt her.

"I wasn't aware that mortals even liked to bathe. You all always smell so foul."

Auren looked amused but saddened when Orien said, "That's because you've only been around the common folk. They do not have the opportunities that we do here. They have your kingdom to thank for their downtrodden state."

Saiph's starfire burned through her veins at the insult. "And how," she asked with false politeness, battling for control she had never bothered to master, "did you come to that conclusion, mortal?"

Orien raised a cool brow at her, indifferent to her anger. Foolish, the men were often more brash than the women. He would be ash on the air faster than he could take his next breath if she so desired. "The constant attacks? The townsfolk are forever building and then re-building when errant starfire wipes out their homes over and over again. Do you not wonder why it is the common folk despise you? Do you think it is fear? It's not. It is bitterness."

Saiph didn't believe what Orien was saying for a single moment, but even so… "What attacks?"

Orien's eyes bulged out and he stood there, mouth hanging open, until Auren smoothly cut-in, easing between them when Saiph hadn't even noticed she had begun to close the distance. "Around once a month, starfire falls to the Earth in targeted bursts. It devastates life wherever it touches. The last attack was four nights ago."

Four nights ago. Just before Saiph arrived. "Do they always occur at the same time each month?" she asked as casually as possible. Saiph didn't believe them, not without proof, but her mother was a devious woman. Cruel, even. There were whispers that the starfire coursing through her had burned away her soul —whispers that perhaps Saiph and Vala hadn't quite discouraged.

Auren's dark eyes flickered with repressed flames as they studied Saiph, and she could have sworn a tendril of heat brushed through her body. Saiph narrowed her eyes at the witch. Had she just tested Saiph with her magick?

"Yes," Auren said at last. "The attacks have been charted. We usually try and evacuate villages where possible, but there's no way of telling exactly where the starfire will strike each time."

Terrorised. That's what Auren and Orien were saying to her. Their people were being terrorised—and Saiph had a good idea as to why: a deterrent. The kingdom fired upon the mortals just before the timeline divergence each month, ensuring they would keep in line and distracted while the kingdom couldn't track their movements. Ironically, if what Auren was saying was true, it meant the humans had a fairly accurate chart of when the monthly timeline divergence began.

Saiph did not particularly care for the mortals, but she also did not abide by unjust suffering. Besides, giving their enemy a map to the kingdom's weakness had to end. "I did not authorise any such attacks. They will be ceased."

Orien sneered at her words, but Auren just continued to study Saiph's face, a small smile playing about her lips, as if she had suspected what Saiph would say from the moment they had told her about it. "See that they do. I know it will curry favour with our queen."

Saiph rolled her eyes. "I will do so because it is what is just. I care not for the favour of a lying mortal."

Orien growled and Auren laid one hand on his arm, stilling him instantly as his eyes continued to burn into Saiph. "A star that cares about justice—now I've heard it all."

"You mortals know nothing of justice, nor honour." Saiph flashed her fangs again, lest he forget exactly who and what she was. Her fangs weren't something she usually had out. It was considered rude to have them on display in the Kingdom of Stars. There was something... freeing about having them visible here. She was different, and she didn't care if they liked it. Saiph decided that from now on, she wouldn't hide them again. She was dangerous, savage, and beautiful —they should not forget it.

Auren was smiling again by the time they reached the bathing area, though Saiph hadn't the faintest clue as to why.

Saiph was expecting a room filled with buckets,

maybe a measly bar of soap. What she found instead left her gaping. It was gorgeous. As gorgeous as any of the night skies in the kingdom. On the other side of the heavy, beige burlap curtain covering the entrance was baths. A natural cavern in the rock surrounded them, filled with holes of varying sizes containing hot springs, judging by the steam that filled the air. It also told Saiph that though they appeared to be underground, they were actually inside the earth. There was no other explanation for the natural recesses. The likelihood was that they were inside a mountain. Possibly several, as some of the tunnels they had walked through seemed man-made, unnaturally smooth, probably a mortal with an affinity for earth magicks. The rocks glowed as if they were filled with stars, illuminating the otherwise dark and steamy space. The skin beneath her breasts immediately became slick with sweat, but Saiph didn't mind. Soon she would be in that blissful water and, with her enhanced healing, she would be good as new in no time. If she was warm, she couldn't imagine how Auren and Orien must have been feeling, but they both looked perfectly collected. No sweat dampened their brows. She supposed this made sense. Auren seemed like the living embodiment of flame, and her brother was made of ice.

Saiph approached the closest wall. It was slick with moisture that ran down in hypnotising rivulets. Peering closer, Saiph started when one of the small stars wriggled.

"What are they?" she whispered, her eyes never leaving the tiny, glowing creature.

Auren moved closer. "Glow-worms. They absorb light and then release it when it's dark."

"I thought they were stars at first," Saiph murmured to herself, reaching out and gently stroking the worm in front of her. It glowed brighter, absorbing some of the light that radiated from her skin. She hardly ever noticed when she was glowing, but a soft, iridescent light was slowly leaking from her. It was different to the harsh glare she had used on the kidnapper in the smuggler's tunnels. Her glamourie was still very much intact, keeping her true glory hidden. Just enough leaked through. Enough to set her apart.

Auren ran her hands through the light escaping Saiph in something like wonder. Her eyes were alight when they met Saiph's. "Beautiful."

Saiph shrugged, feeling hot under Auren's scrutiny. "I am a star. We glow."

"I have not met many stars," Auren said, a rueful smile twisting her mouth to one side as flames speckled with silver rimmed the hands she dragged through Saiph's light once more before they flickered and disappeared. Had the silver tinge been a trick of the light? True starfire glowed blue and silver, and it appeared the witch did not possess enough blood from the stars to conjure more than this, but still, it was interesting that even that much power slept inside the witch's veins. "But

I do not imagine that any others glow quite as you do."

Saiph let her eyes linger on Auren's hands for a moment longer before deciding to voice her question. Who exactly did this false heir have following her? Protecting her? "You are gifted with starfire. How?"

Auren smiled. "Not quite," she said, but elaborated no further. "Come, you should bathe."

Saiph stood stiffly for a moment, jaw clenched as she considered the witch. She could not wring the answers from her by force, not with the bond between them staying her hand. But she would get her answers, one way or another.

Orien, who had been silent during their exchange, stepped forward and led them over to a more secluded bathing hole. "This should do. At least people will have to put some effort in now in order to gawk at you."

Saiph smirked but didn't bother replying, just shucked off her leather bottoms and cotton tunic top in one fast motion, leaving her bare but for her swords which hung from one shoulder in their harness. Orien blinked, his gaze travelling up Saiph's body and then back down again. Saiph raised a brow. Orien was lucky her leather boots had already been removed when she awoke, else he may have fainted when she bent over.

"Good to know you're not shy," Orien muttered but looked oddly like he was trying not to laugh.

"What would I have to be shy about?" Saiph answered with a smirk as she brushed between Orien and Auren and settled into the scalding hot water with a groan. "I don't understand the fascination you mortals have with modesty."

Orien made an odd choking noise and Auren's mouth curled into a sinfully wide smile as her eyes travelled down to Saiph's chest, where her lightly glowing breasts were not quite covered by the frothy water.

"If you're quite done ogling me——" Saiph said, slightly amused but trying to ignore it as the siblings both jumped a little and immediately looked elsewhere. "What will I use to wash with?"

Orien opened his mouth, but Auren beat him to speech. "Orien will bring you a towel and some soap. You can take off your swords, you know. They're getting wet. Nobody here would dare touch them."

Saiph smirked. "Save you, perhaps, and I have many questions about that. If anyone else tried, they would immediately wither away into dust." Nevertheless, she removed the harness and pulled herself from the water to place them on the side of the pool. The blades were ancient and powerful and normally they sang just for her, but Auren eyed them like she could hear the faint whisper of star magick calling as Saiph stepped back. The water glistened on her body, caught in her own glow and enhanced by the glitter of the cave worms. This time, Auren did not look away when Saiph smirked. Instead, she moved to unclasp her golden buckles and shrug out of her long-sleeved, leather protective hyde. Orien grabbed her arm in alarm, but Auren merely shrugged him off with a look that Saiph couldn't read.

Orien rolled his eyes. "I'll be back with the soap and towels."

Auren shrugged out of the leather hyde and pulled the thin tunic top over her head, baring her breasts. She didn't falter, didn't hesitate, moving as confidently as if she were in her most natural state—which to Saiph, she was. Auren's body was curvy, with wide hips and soft thighs. Her stomach, however, was tight with muscle, as if she spent long hours training.

Auren turned and smoothly slid her supple leather bottoms down her legs, the glow-worms casting interestingly patterned light over her darker skin. There, up the side of her thigh to mid-waist snarled a thick, silver scar. Saiph had her own nicks and scars from fighting over the years, but nothing so large or gnarly as Auren's. It spoke of a grave injury, but now did not seem the time to mention it. Nor, Saiph sternly reminded herself, should she care enough to want to ask. *My enemy,* she thought firmly.

"May I join you?" Auren asked softly as she stood naked before the pool. Her arms were at her sides, hiding nothing. Her scars glinted proudly in the glow-light, a testament to her strength, her endurance. Auren let Saiph look her fill before raising a brow in a haughty imitation of Saiph herself. She almost laughed. Almost.

"You may," Saiph answered, drifting backwards to the far-side of the pool as Auren climbed in, her heavy breasts floating in the water for a moment as she sank in, the peachy tips visible for only a second before the darkness of the water covered her fully.

"We are not your enemies, you know."

Saiph said nothing, looking once more at the glow-worms. They both knew that wasn't true.

"What I mean to say is, the Kingdom of Stars has been no friend to us, to our people. But it does not have to remain so."

Saiph slowly turned to look back at Auren. "What you speak of is treason. To both your false queen and my own."

Auren raised her brows. "And agreeing to work with us is not? Tell me, *seren*, how will your mother feel about this alliance you have made?" Auren murmured silkily.

The truth was that her mother would not know, the disparity between timelines by now so out of sync that the human realm was completely unsupervised—save for Saiph, of course. She couldn't tell Auren that though. Undoubtedly, she would go running to the false heir and they would gather all the magic they could and strike at the stars. It was what she would do in Auren's place, even if it wouldn't work.

"I am the heir to the throne. I will do as I see fit. My queen understands the severity of a blood debt. Make no mistake, once our debt is settled, I will turn this place into so much dust."

Auren smirked, as if she had expected such an answer. "Yes, I'm sure you rather think you might."

Saiph didn't bother to reply and Orien came strolling towards them at that moment anyway, bearing soap. Another mortal male walked at his side, carrying the towels. He was tall, Saiph could make out very little of his face in the darkness from so far away. All she could see was the occasional flash of red hair as they passed a cluster of glow-worms.

"So this is her," the man said as they reached the edge of the pool and set the towels and soap down. He gave a nod to Auren and then stepped back to further analyse Saiph.

"And who might you be?" she asked in her most disinterested and cold voice, flashing a little fang for good measure.

"Raze," he said, no ruffles, no nonsense, not cowed in the slightest. "Advisor to the queen."

"Mm, nobody important then."

A muscle ticked in Orien's pale jaw, and Saiph bit back her laugh. It was too easy to provoke him. It almost wasn't any fun.

Raze didn't so much as react though, just met Saiph's dark eyes with his hazel ones and nodded. "Indeed, so it would seem." It almost sounded like a reprimand and Orien winced, scrubbing his hand over his jaw.

"Ah, I'm guessing my stay wasn't wholly approved, then," Saiph said with a smirk as she stood from the water and let it cascade down her slim, lithe body as she stepped close to Auren. Raze and Orien both tensed, but Saiph only smirked and reached for the soap in Auren's hand, wrapping her glowing fingers around Auren's and then letting go in a glide of skin that had Saiph's breasts tightening. Auren's gaze dropped and embers flashed in her eyes before fading so quickly Saiph questioned whether they had truly been there at all.

"Tell me, how does one become a queen without a throne?" Saiph idly drew the soap over her skin and raised her pale arm up into the air once it was free of blood.

"Much the same way a pretender steals one, I suppose," Orien growled out, and Saiph frowned, unsure what he was referring to.

"Is there something you needed, Raze?" asked Auren, interrupting before Saiph could retort, and moving closer to the edge of the pool.

"The queen has requested your presence," Raze murmured, casting his shadowed gaze to where Saiph swam lazily, pausing to lather and then repeat, secure in the fact that she was the biggest predator there and, as such, had nothing to fear. Auren, perhaps, might be a match. She was still too unknown to say for sure, but she seemed more likely to bed Saiph than kill her.

Auren nodded as if she had been expecting this. "Tell her I'm on my way."

Raze nodded and turned and left without another word or even a glance in Saiph's direction.

She grinned into the darkness, her head cradled by the water as she floated on her back and admired the glow-worms in the ceiling. It was almost as if she could be floating in the night sky. "In my experience, it is often worse to ask for forgiveness than permission."

Orien snorted, but Auren said nothing as Saiph dipped her head beneath the water briefly before pushing onto her back and floating.

The slosh of water disturbed her thoughts as Auren climbed out of the bath and into the waiting towel that Orien held out. "You may wander where you wish," Auren said as she wiped the beads of water from her arms and wrung out her long hair, so heavy with water it looked almost black.

"Aren't you concerned I'll escape?"

"Not even slightly," Auren said with a cunning gleam in her eye. "You could search every nook of the caverns and still not find the way out. Besides, I'm certain you wouldn't renege on our bargain. We both know the consequences wouldn't be pleasant."

It was the first time Auren had admitted to knowing more than she should, but Saiph didn't pounce on it. Instead, she gave a smile that was more fang than pleasantry.

"Perhaps you are right… but the stars always know how to find the sky."

Auren carefully wrapped and knotted the cloth towel around her body, the material turning dark in interesting places where the water still clung. "Then I wish you luck, little star. But I do not think it is the sky that you truly call home."

Saiph's body jerked in surprise, and she inelegantly flailed her arms to keep from going under as she spluttered. "Oh? You do not think the heir to the throne of the Kingdom of Stars calls the night sky home?"

"No," Auren said simply. Her skin had begun to pebble with gooseflesh, and Saiph forcefully tore her gaze away.

"*No*?" Saiph repeated. "Then where, exactly, do you think I belong?"

Auren turned away. Orien waited for her by the burlap curtained entrance to the baths, tapping his foot impatiently.

"You belong to the wilds, *seren*," she murmured over her shoulder, quiet enough that only Saiph's ears would be able to pick it up, and then disappeared through the curtain Orien held open.

Her words seemed to ripple through the waters in the many pools as Saiph remained floating, her skin cooling despite the steam as she hesitantly tucked the words around the weak light of her heart.

The wilds.

CHAPTER FIVE
EIGHTY-FOUR YEARS PREVIOUSLY

THE COTTAGE HAD BEEN EMPTY WHEN AGATHA returned just after dusk, her basket heavy with berries and a melody caught on her tongue. They had fled here on the night of the King's death and had yet to leave the Forest's protective shroud. Even the stars couldn't best old magick. Agatha had watched the babes grow, weathered their incessant questions and wonderings of their patronage, their fates. *Soon*, she had told them, *all will be explained soon*, and they had settled for the small bits of information they could coax out of her.

They had found the cottage nestled neatly between tall trees and surrounded by berry bushes, well-kept and beckoning. The Forest had clearly decided to take fate into its own hands, and Agatha could only bring herself to be grateful for that fact. She had ventured outside of the Forest on occasion, usually for food as the children could not get sick—not with their heritage.

But she kept these excursions infrequent and short, not wanting to leave the twins alone for too long lest they get up to all sorts of mischief.

Agatha approached the cottage slowly, the basket so full she had to waddle to carry it, and immediately had the sense that something was amiss. Over the years, she'd long learned to listen to her instincts. The Forest protected them, sheltered them, but it too was home to creatures of the unforgiving sort.

She walked inside and paused at the threshold warily. It was too still. The dust had begun to settle in the air, and the fire had long burned out. The basket fell from her grip, black berries smashing to leave bloody smears on the rough wooden floor as she spun on her feet to look back out at the dark trees. Where were the twins?

Every now and then, it felt like she could hear the Forest. Felt it guiding her or prodding her despite that she had no magick of her own, save the spark that granted her life, as all mortals had. It was as if the longer she remained inside the darkness, the more in tune with it she became.

"Fools," she hissed as she stalked forward, dark cloak whirling about her as she pulled it up and over her head, feeling the prodding of the Forest as it encouraged her to find her charges. They could wander where they willed, so long as they remained inside the protection of the trees. Most of what they had needed the Forest had provided. Each short trip she had made to the local town made her heart pound, certain the village folk would sense something amiss. Worse, she would hear the dark whispers that flitted from mouth to mouth, encouraged by the murderous Queen of the Stars no doubt, that the king and queen had been poisoned by human rebels, their heirs slaughtered while they slept. *Lies.* Twisted and thorny, Agatha had known where they had been spindled and that they must be warier than ever to not attract the attention of the skies, biting her tongue as the truth longed to spill free.

The Forest beckoned her, dark shadows swirling and tugging at her hem, pulling at her ankles and clasping at her breath. Agatha had warned the twins— the Forest's protection extended only so far. In leaving, they would be untenably vulnerable. She hadn't fled in the middle of the night, sacrificed her home and everything she knew for a life of seclusion and secrecy just for the children to die now — and the hope for their stolen kingdom with them.

The wind breathed down her neck and spurred her legs faster. The heavy steps sank her into mulch and mud but she pushed through, relentless. Knowing if she did not then all she fought for was at risk. The deepness of the sky began to lighten, an unnatural white growing as if summoning mist from the clouds themselves, and dread curdled in Agatha's stomach as she hurried to the edge of the Forest. The sound of laughter hit her ears hard and momentarily froze her in her tracks.

"What by the *stars above* do you think you are doing!"

The children froze, laughter dying on their lips and wilting on their faces. The boy stepped forward. "Oh please Aggie, don't be angry. We only wanted to step outside for a moment and watch the sun. There is only darkness within the Forest. We tire of it."

She had been too soft on the children. Though, admittedly, they were not so young anymore. She should have been tougher. Done more to prepare them for what now lay in wait.

The girl looked at her, deep eyes wide and face solemn. "I'm sorry, Aggie. It was my idea. What could be the harm in it?"

The sky flashed and the girl jumped, huddling closer to her brother.

"We must leave. Now. Back to the cottage, quickly."

Two stubborn chin lifts met her words, and Agatha shuddered as the sky went white once more.

"If you accompany me now, I will give you the answers you have long since sought. I swear it."

"Why not now?" the boy asked sullenly, all traces of laughter firmly wiped away.

Agatha ran a gnarled hand through her greying hair in frustration, cursing as her fingers became entangled in a wind knot. "Because if we do not leave now, the Queen of Stars will get what she's wanted since she killed your parents. Your deaths."

The paleness of the air seemed to seep into the faces of the children, leaving them looking like wraiths beneath the fringe of leaves, but still, they did not move.

"We have hidden," Agatha began, knowing they would not move unless she gave them something, anything, "because you are a threat. One the *Domitor* will not abide. The Forest is old magick, do you recall? Have you not heard it whisper? Its magick shields us, for the *Domitor* cannot see you through its shroud."

The children looked at her with disbelieving eyes, rounded with confusion. Thunder rumbled loudly, rattling her bones and setting her teeth on edge. It was the girl who took the first step back towards safety, leaves rustling underfoot that whispered to Agatha in words the children felt but could not glean.

"We are too late," Agatha said softly, knowing the truth of it in her soul, her breath shivering through the air in a cloud of resignation. The last of the moonlight cupped her face and the girl span to her brother with her hand outstretched, almost in slow motion. Agatha knew what must be done, just as she had all those years ago when she swept two babes from their cradles, her fate inextricably twined with theirs.

The boy's eyes met hers in shock as he found her suddenly in front of him. "Run," she breathed and threw her arms wide as a bolt of pure starfire swept down from the sky towards them. The darkness of the Forest seemed to cringe away from it, as though relinquishing its protection to huddle in around itself. "RUN!" Agatha screamed as she took the bolt, bore the pain as she would have done a thousand times over to see her kingdom back to rightness. With her skin crawling, hair catching, and ash smouldering in her throat, she sank to the ground and felt only relief as the Forest sheltered the children once more. Swallowing them up in protective darkness, so deep the starlight could not shine.

Her skin writhed with heat, but Agatha let her lips tug into one last taut smile as she rolled on her back to look up at the sky.

"*Victor,*" she breathed, "*Victor Victis.*"

The *Domitor* Queen would not keep her seat for long.

CHAPTER SIX
SAIPH

"THIS IS YOUR PLAN?" SAIPH STARED ACROSS THE rough-hewn wooden table at Orien, whose icy blues followed every twitch of her muscles. She might have been flattered if not for the fact she knew he had more interest in killing her than fucking her. "Forgive me for not being overly confident in your brother's ability to be... subtle."

Orien's scowl somehow grew fouler, and his hand seemed to gravitate automatically to the blade at his hip. Saiph flashed her fangs at him and he threw it, faster than she had expected but still so slow, so mortal. She barely caught the blade before she whipped it back at him with force and then hissed as a feeling of electricity shot over her hand painfully, the dagger flying awry.

Auren's full mouth twitched, but her composure held as she looked at the blade quivering in the dirt wall next to her brother's head. "Unfortunately, the source we need can be elusive. Orien is best-suited to tracking them."

Saiph glared at the dagger before begrudgingly looking back toward the witch. She had not thought to bargain for her own safety when they had struck the deal, but Saiph found she didn't mind. A little pain made things more fun. "You do know that we *both* have obligations as part of this blood debt? Including your need to provide me with the opportunity to fulfil it." Saiph unfolded her legs blindingly fast and settled them back onto the ground, relishing the way Orien jumped when he abruptly found her face a hairsbreadth from his own. Yes, she could not kill him. Yet. But the hunt could be just as thrilling. "So don't skimp on the details, little *ignis*. I'll have your last blood in my mouth one way or the other. Soon."

Auren quirked her brows and shot Orien a quick look. Saiph let out a hiss of laughter when she saw another dagger clasped firmly in his hand. He blinked and cursed, sliding it away quickly as he avoided her gaze.

"If you will have our last blood regardless, then what is the harm in humouring our little plan for now, *seren?* I swear upon my blood and breath that this is no trick. Ren truly does have the best hope of finding our source. They're remarkably skittish and have considerable skill in remaining undetected. If they do not want to be found, then they won't be."

Saiph had never met the animal she couldn't hunt. She'd even found the rebels eventually – though this was admittedly through fate as much as skill. "If they are as elusive as you say, then how will your brother be any better at hunting them than I?"

A flicker of a grin brushed Auren's mouth, tugging at her scar and turning it white. "It is a familiar task for my brother, and not an entirely unwelcome chase."

Now Saiph was truly disbelieving. Who, by the stars above, could possibly *want* to be chased by Orien? Though, Saiph might be partial to a chase herself... so long as it ended with her fangs in his throat. She let the savage grin the thoughts inspired part her lips, and Orien whitened once more at the sight of her teeth. Why had she ever hidden them before? The stars considered it in bad taste to have them on display, typically they were reserved for hunting, fucking, or the slightly rarer ceremony of mating. If Saiph was lucky, she might yet get to experience both of the former in her time on the mortal plane. She flicked a glance between the siblings and let her grin widen—there would be no doubt as to who would play what role.

Orien stood abruptly, as if having seen enough of her face to last him a lifetime. "Well, there's no point in delaying any further. If we want to have a hope of finding these men before they take any others, then we must move fast."

"Hopefully your mysterious 'source' has as much underground knowledge as you hope."

Auren stood, embracing her brother tightly and murmuring something in his ear so low that Saiph could not parse it. "Be safe, brother. Send my love."

Orien nodded back, throwing Saiph a look of venom before scooping up his satchel and rushing through the curtained door. Auren stared after him wistfully for a moment before sighing. "Follow me."

No room for argument. A demand, sheer and brazen. Nobody ever directed her as such, except her mother, perhaps.

Saiph sketched a mocking bow and was surprised at the ire that tightened Auren's jaw, her eyes burning brighter as if in defiance. It was gone in a blink as Saiph straightened, watching her warily. A smirk curled the edges of Auren's mouth, her tongue flicking out from between her parted lips as she purred, "Now *seren*, let's not be hasty. If you wish to worship me on your knees, I wouldn't say no."

Saiph could only blink in surprise. A flash of her fangs could make Orien balk, but nothing she did seemed to phase this woman. The more savage Saiph became, the more Auren seemed to delight in her. It was… inconvenient.

"Why do you say such things to me?"

"What—are you too good to bed a human? Or is it that you are royalty, your Highness?"

"It is that I am a star, and I have yet to decide which would be more pleasurable—to kill you slowly or fast. Besides, it is forbidden."

Auren's smirk widened. "Scared, *seren*?"

"I do not fear that which I could so easily kill."

"There is more to life than death, Saiph."

It was the first time the witch had said her name. The sound of it prickled unpleasantly against her skin and tightened the space between her brows into a frown.

"Quite, witch."

"Come, I only meant to show you to your quarters."

Saiph followed slowly as Auren pressed out of the suddenly oppressive room, prowling deeper within the mountain caves. "Did your people create these tunnels?" Her own voice echoed around them and Saiph's breath caught, reminded of another time underground, deeper than anything the mortals could conceive. A different, more alive dark peering back at her, a shocking hollow where any light simply ceased to be, her soul swallowed whole.

A warm hand clasped her elbow, and Saiph hissed, jolting back and bumping into the dirt wall. Auren stared at her, unphased and likely unaware of how close to death she had just been as small trickles of earth fell around Saiph. Trapped in the recesses of her mind as she had been, Saiph couldn't speak to what she would or would not do.

"Yes," Auren said curtly, startling Saiph momentarily. "We have some here who are gifted with the earth and were able to create most of what we have here."

Saiph nodded, grateful when Auren turned around once more and continued down the dimly lit tunnel without another word. Saiph did not fear the dark, for it usually reminded her of her twin. But she did not trust this place, rife with cunning mortals.

"What occupies your thoughts, *seren?*" Auren's throaty voice wrapped around her like a live thing, warm and enticing—dangerous.

"How right my mother was about the repulsive nature of you mortals." One moment her foot hovered mid-air, ready to take its next step, and the next she was pinned to the wall once more, though this time not by the force of her own memories. Not a muscle gave, thanks to the arm slapped across her chest, and when Saiph looked up, shocked into silence and immobility, she was stunned by the flames that swirled in Auren's eyes. Oranges and reds intertwined with blazing silver, curling languidly then spinning faster and faster in time with Auren's breath.

"You know nothing of us." The witch's voice was deep and husky with a darkness Saiph had yet to hear from her, even trapped and blood-soaked in that smuggler's tunnel. "It is easy to rule from afar, never seeing your subjects. It is no wonder we follow a new queen. A *just* queen." Anger began to curl in Saiph's stomach, turning to lead as Auren continued on. "One who does not burn her people to ashes over and over, lets them re-build *over and over*, just to snatch away their hope like starlight spinning away on a breeze."

She was right. Her mother was not a *just* queen. In fact, she had no interest in justice at all, especially not for the mortals. It wasn't a stance Saiph necessarily agreed with… but it was not her place to question her mother.

A stuttered half a heartbeat passed, and then Auren's voice found her once more in the ensuing silence. The arm like a vise across Saiph's chest trembled lightly as Auren whispered, "I do not believe you to be so cruel." Her voice was like silk but poised to strike, like a knife balanced en-pointe.

"That is because you do not know me at all."

"Do I not? I have bled with you, I have fought for you, I have seen your scars both inner and outer."

"That," Saiph said, voice as gentle as she could make it to prevent a further lapse in Auren's fiery temper, "tells me far more about you than it does you, me."

A husky laugh stirred the fine hairs above Saiph's ear, Auren's mouth, hauntingly close to her throat. A wildness zipped through Saiph as a flicker of warm breath teased her skin—wondering for just a moment, no more, what it might be like if Auren were truly her match, able to sink in her own fangs.

"Maybe so, but I do not believe you heartless—unlike my brother, who cannot go two breaths without baring his blade in your presence. He doesn't trust you."

Saiph smirked. Provoking Orien was truly too easy. Auren's words cut through the lingering desire muddling her senses. All she longed for now was the sky and rest. Though, thankfully, she needed far less of it than a typical mortal, but it had been an especially trying day — or was it now two? After using both her flames and then the blood loss, she would definitely need to recharge tonight. It would have been better if she could do so beneath the starlight, but she suspected that wouldn't be possible this deep within the mountain. She made to push away from the wall but found herself still held in place.

"And you? Do you trust me?" Saiph would think Auren a fool if she did.

"Not yet, *seren*, but I do not fear you either."

Saiph considered Auren in the cover of darkness, the smoothness of her brow and the focus of her gaze, tested herself against the strength that held her immobile and raised a brow. "How are you doing this?"

Auren waved her question off, moving away from her but not allowing them to proceed any further. "I am no fool. If I felt you were truly a danger to anyone here, you would be dead. I guard the lost crown, the people... I would not gamble with their lives. I also," Auren tipped a crooked smile her way, as if knowing Saiph could see her despite the darkness, "consider myself an excellent judge of character. I grew up with Orien—I can spot a lie a mile away. So tell me. Why pretend? Why spout that vitriol as if it were your own truth? Did you seek to provoke me?"

Indecision flared in Saiph's gut, tightening and churning as her heart quickened. Telling this truth could be a risk. Regardless of her private concerns over her mother's ruthless rule, this witch was her enemy, and she could not weaken her mother in such a way as to confide in a stranger. "Why would I care to provoke you?"

Auren slid a step closer once more and her eyes seemed darker, like they had taken in the depths surrounding them and claimed them for her own. "I think we both know the answer to that."

Attraction was a pretty bargaining chip, but it alone was not enough to convince Saiph that she should reveal this potentially lethal truth. "I'm afraid you have overestimated your mortal allure, Auren."

Saiph blinked, and the witch was at her throat once more. The arm across her chest softened to become an invitation, and warm air stirred across the skin at the hollow of her jaw as a featherlight brush of lips pressed there momentarily.

"Have I?" Auren said huskily, and the beast within Saiph surged up unexpectedly. Her fangs ached as if they were trying to lengthen further in an effort to reach the little witch, whose eyes now glinted at her in challenge. Saiph felt dizzy with confusion and desire. What was happening to her? She had taken lovers in the past, but none had affected her as Auren now did —was it some kind of mortal magick? A spell? The blood bond?

As quickly as the questions appeared, they slipped away, something inside her seeming to draw closer to the witch without Saiph's permission.

Who would know? What would really be the harm in admitting this small flaw? Her mother could not see her now thanks to the timeline divergence. Anything she spoke would likely remain here in the darkness of these caves. Yet, Auren may see it as a weakness, some sort of softening or fondness to exploit. Starlight knew her twin had worried as much. It was what made Saiph's task so deliciously ironic, unbeknownst to Saiph's mother, of course. Kill the mortals Saiph had grown to enjoy watching. To see them persevere and struggle and love seemingly endlessly, though their short lives flickered and guttered like the bright flash of a flame. Their brief existences were nothing in the face of starlight, of immortality, yet still they toiled on.

"It is what's expected," Saiph said once she felt it was safe enough to open her mouth without sinking her fangs. Let Auren think what she may. Perhaps it would aid Saiph in her quest to find and kill the mortal heir if the little witch thought her soft, sympathetic.

"You do not hate us."

Saiph said nothing. She would do as her Queen bade her regardless of any hate—why Auren pushed to hear her say it she didn't know. It made no difference.

"Why does your queen bother?" Saiph sighed quietly, letting her breath soak into the dirt that blanketed all other noise, muffling their footsteps as Auren stepped back and finally allowed them to continue on the pathway. "What is there left for her to fight for?"

"There are the people."

"Barely. They will be dust on the wind sooner rather than later."

"You have seen only the worst the kingdom has to offer. Camber is the worst of us, but there are still wonders left in our world yet, contrary to what you have seen. Towns like Camber have been hit the hardest, have to do the most re-builds. Often the townsfolk just move on to the next town and the next, until there are no more, all of them reduced to so much rubble."

Camber had to be the mortal encampment she had passed through on her first days on this plane. Saiph raised an eyebrow in the dark. "You knew where I was?"

Auren's eyes crinkled at the corners as she shot Saiph a wry look. "A star walks the earth for the first time in years and you think I wouldn't be watching? I'm the queen's guard. Of course I knew where you were."

Saiph laughed shortly. "Yet, you claim to have no ideas on the men who captured us? If you were watching me, surely you saw their faces."

"They saw me long before I noticed them. I had my eyes trained on what I perceived to be the bigger threat. How do you think I got caught?"

At this Saiph laughed truly. "Snagged while ogling the star."

Auren laughed under her breath.

"You knew what I was. Before I awoke in the caves and revealed myself. Why bring me here? What game are you playing, Auren?" Saiph's voice was a caress in the dark, a gauntlet and a mark. A truth for a truth—it would be a fair bargain. Just what was this mortal really capable of?

Auren's eyes flared brightly once more, and her mouth clamped shut as a wave of heat swam off the witch's form, raising the fine hair on Saiph's arms. She laughed breathlessly as the little witch began to come undone once more. She hadn't realised it was such an important question, but now she realised she would need to find out the answer soon, to protect herself and her kingdom both.

"I am here for more than just a blood debt, am I not?"

The rising warmth vanished at her voice, like a candle extinguished, and Saiph bit back her growl of disappointment. Auren's head was tilted downwards and Saiph moved forward, reaching with a single digit, glowing against the pitch black, to raise her chin, when Auren's head snapped up and she continued on like nothing had passed.

There was a grace to her movements that hadn't been there before, a sway to her hips that called to domination, and Saiph wondered where Auren could have pushed all that burning power—and what would happen when she exploded?

"Here," Auren said curtly a few minutes later. She brushed aside a curtain made of soft material and swept into a small, dark room. The floor was dusty from the compacted dirt, but there was a bed standing in the middle of the room and an oil lantern beside it on the ground. Saiph made her way to the bed and sat gingerly on the edge of the threadbare mattress. It looked hardly better than the dirt floor.

"Forgive me," Auren rasped suddenly and Saiph's head snapped up in alarm, looking for a weapon, some sort of indication of treachery. Back-stabbing bastards, mortals, she couldn't forget it for a second. The stars had already paid too high a price for such forgetfulness once before.

But Auren's eyes were a warm, sincere, gold once more when they met her own. No sign of the slumbering power that lurked within, nor the impressive strength that had held even Saiph in place. It was now clear why this woman had been chosen for the heir's guard. She was more than just her flames.

"You're right. You're here for more than just the blood debt... when I brought you here, I wished to know what kind of leader you would be. The people here are my duty, mine and my queen's. The people of this kingdom... the people in these caves, have seen more hardship and sorrow than they ever deserved. Perhaps you care not. They are not truly your people, are they—despite that you will one day rule them." Saiph stared at Auren, at the genuine concern in her eyes, belied by the tight curl of her mouth. In truth, Saiph had not thought about what it meant to be heir other than in regards to the stars. "You are not what I expected. It was a snap decision in the smuggler's tunnels to bring you here, and the blood debt ensured our safety while I ascertained exactly what manner of monster we may soon have on the throne."

"Angling for advisor to the true heir apparent, witch?" Saiph lounged back on the hard bed, the picture of ease, and slipped a dagger free from her boot, twirling it between her fingers with ease.

"Something like that."

Saiph sat up slowly but knew the witch was gone without needing to see it for herself. The room fell silent and the darkness bled in once more, as if it had been waiting, lurking until Auren's heat had left, leaving Saiph vulnerable once more. It pulsed around her in time with her heartbeats, throbbing through her skin and into her fangs, and she retracted them as quickly as she could. Saiph had been in the mortal world for no more than a week and was already unravelling. Working with mortals, breaking the covenants…

The sky is but a whisper away.

It felt further than a mere whisper, and Saiph's hands ached at her sides as she spun her dagger faster and faster until the blade plunged into her palm and Saiph breathed deeply at last. Letting the pain cut through the tinge of panic that shot through her, colouring her breaths and tightening her stomach. The earth. It was the one thing she could not abide. How could she be expected to rule this place that so easily sent her back into that impenetrable darkness? She needed to remember her people, her duty.

As Auren's words rang round and round in Saiph's head, she considered that she may have more than one duty, more than one people to bear responsibility for.

"...*exactly what manner of monster we may soon have on the throne.*"

Soon. *Soon.* What did Auren know that made her think she needed to safeguard her queen closer than ever? To prepare for a new ruler on the throne? More than that, what had she been prepared to do if Saiph had been more the monster she was expecting?

Decision made, Saiph slunk out of bed and towards the curtain waving softly in a breeze that seemed to perpetually chase through the halls. It was time to look for the illustrious heir.

CHAPTER SEVEN
SAIPH

Saiph had spent the entire night searching, unable to quell her restless thoughts as she prowled the corridors with her senses alert. She had run into very few people and, to her surprise, those she had barely spared her a glance. In honesty, she was a little... offended. These people hadn't seen a star possibly ever in their lifetime, and she hadn't even been worth a second look. It felt like she was missing something. Truly the only person in this star-forsaken rebel camp who actually seemed to fear her was Orien—it was unnerving. What did they know that she didn't?

More than unnerving, it was *insulting* that they weren't even attempting to watch her. Hadn't even bothered to give her a guard! Or perhaps they were foolish, or thought her to be safe, a monster de-clawed because of her blood debt to Auren. Saiph let out a snort that echoed through the tunnels and sent a shiver of sweat down her spine. She quickly shook the anxiety away. There was no greater predator than her down here, and she would not be trapped forever. Her long legs ate up the space as she searched a different branch of the caves, stopping as voices began to sound in the distance. The humans were a way off yet, and she strained to catch the fleeting sounds of their conversation.

"Have you seen her?"

A short laugh and a deep voice replied, "How could I not? Stalking around at all hours of the night."

Were they talking about her? A little reckless given their knowledge of her fondness for *stalking around at all hours of the night*. Their footsteps were echoing as they moved closer to where Saiph stood quietly in the tunnel, the sound of their heartbeats a siren's call as they thudded, thudded, thudded close. Achingly close. Her mouth filled with saliva, and she knew that if she could check her eyes would be black. Bloodlust had never been an issue for her in the Kingdom of Stars— then again, nobody there irritated her quite as much as these mortals.

Saiph breathed in slowly and started to retreat when the men's conversation stilled her once more.

"Auren is a fool to bring her here. This isn't going to work, especially considering—"

A hand closed on her elbow and Saiph jumped, so engrossed in the conversation that she hadn't even noticed someone coming up behind her. It was the fox all over again! Saiph spun around quickly, grabbing onto the hand as she moved and heard the

84

scuffling of feet as the men approaching heard the commotion.

It was the man, the advisor to the heir, Raze. His eyes stared at her steadily, and she dropped his hand from her bone-crushing grip swiftly. He didn't curse or act like anything was wrong, just continued his watchful silence as the men skidded to a stop a few metres away.

Raze's eyes flicked away from her to chastise the men, boys, really, now that Saiph could see them, and they shuffled their feet guilty as they glanced over at her and away again like frightened mice eager to scurry away. Her eyes returned to Raze as she stepped back. Had he been following her?

"I don't need a babysitter," Saiph said and then whirled to face the boys, pushing past them and continuing on as her mind tried to digest what she had managed to overhear. It seemed like Auren had more clout here than she let on if she had managed to persuade the heir that Saiph should stay. But why? It had to be more than just risk analysis. She could have done that from afar. What did the witch want from her?

"I suppose I imagined you salivating earlier then," Raze said dryly as he fell into step beside her. Fuck. He *had* been following her.

"Yes, well, it's a bit of a culture shock coming to this plane. I didn't expect you all to smell quite so much."

Raze's eyebrows rose, but a slither of humour

tugged at his mouth. "Apologies, I'll see if we can do something about the... smell."

Saiph froze between steps with her foot hovering just above the ground as warmth, coppery and rich, slid through her, whispering as it lured her closer, to drink, to take, to claim.

This time when Raze's hand shot out to hold her still, she did not hesitate. The crack of his wrist bone echoed sharply through the tunnels, but Saiph was deaf to it, lost to the hunger and the hunt. She didn't remember moving, but suddenly her presence was looming within an open doorway, one she hadn't seen before.

A deep, thick red was spreading across the dirt floor and Saiph's hands shook from need. But she wouldn't scrabble in the dirt like an animal. No, she deserved straight from the source. Her nostrils flared as she brought the scent in deep, feeling her gums ache and her throat catch aflame with thirst. What was this hunger? She hadn't felt it since she was a child and her magic had begun to emerge.

"Saiph."

Her name made her pause. Who could know her here? Who would dare intervene? She hadn't realised her eyes had slipped closed, but now they fluttered open to meet gold. Auren.

"Saiph," she said again. "*Seren,*" she called. Her jaw was clenched tight, and there was a power in her voice that Saiph hadn't heard before. Auren's hands were clenched at her side and smears of blood ran up her arms, a queasy feeling took root in Saiph's gut.

"Are you hurt?" Saiph asked, finally able to speak past the hunger demanding that she rip and tear.

"No," Auren said gently, but Saiph knew she was holding something back. It was there in the flicker of her eyes as they darted away from her and back again, in the paleness of the scar that slashed through her mouth.

Senses roaring, the bond tugged her forward until she grasped one of Auren's bloody arms between her fingers. "Who did this to you?"

Auren pulled her arm free with ease but said nothing, and Saiph couldn't hold back the snarl that rumbled through the room. Curse this fucking bond, making her feel this unbearable need to *protect*. She had mistakenly thought that agreeing not to harm Auren or those under her protection meant just that, not that Saiph would be compelled to tear anyone else to pieces if they dared harm her. This would be problematic. She needed to break this bond, and soon, if she had any hope of fulfilling her mission.

Breathing shallowly, Saiph assessed the room... and the body. There was a white woman huddled in the corner with her two young children. Her face was pale, but her arms were corded with tension as she forcefully pressed the children's gaze into her chest and away from the body of what Saiph could only assume to be their father.

"What happened?"

Auren opened her mouth, but a deep voice cut her off before she could speak.

"Well, this *is* a surprise."

Saiph turned slowly, keeping her breathing light to avoid slipping back into that same fervour from before. A man stood staring at her as if she were a fascinating new development and not the harbinger of his death. Clasped in the man's arms, with a blade pressed to his throat, was a small boy. His eyes were wet, but the set of his mouth told her he was brave, so she smiled at the child, hardly more than a babe surely, and saw the resolve in his face strengthen.

"I wish I could say the same," Saiph said silkily, straightening from the slight crouch she had assumed to get a better look at the boy. His olive skin was pale, like it might have bronzed if given the opportunity to see sunlight, and Saiph felt a stab of unexpected pity for the mortals forced to live here for a semblance of normalcy. The man holding the boy was unremarkable, white, brown hair, brown eyes, and an unshaved scruff hiding the majority of his lower face. "Yet, unfortunately, this is the least surprising thing you could have done for a human male. Knife to throat?" Saiph tutted slowly as she took one solitary step forward and saw the man's pupils dilate. "How cliché."

The man gave a harsh swallow that sounded loud in the small room, even to Saiph's ears. Lantern light played across his dirty face, and Saiph watched his hand tighten on the blade clutched in his fist. One wrong move and the boy would be dead.

"Saiph," Auren cautioned as Saiph moved another half a step closer. Saiph ignored her.

"What is it you've come here for, little man? Death?"

The young boy had begun to tremble, and a small bead of blood built and slipped down his throat. She couldn't stop her eyes from following its progress as anger began a slow simmer in her stomach. More than anything else, young were to be protected, treasured. In the Kingdom of Stars they were often hard to come by, and to endanger one so recklessly, even if he was a copper-a-dozen mortal... It raged against all of her instincts, everything she had been raised to believe. Even if the bond did not demand it, the man had secured his death the moment that blade had kissed the babe's neck.

"I've come to kill the heir."

"Then we are aligned, for I, too, wish to kill the heir."

The man's brows rose, and his grip loosed on the knife ever so slightly. She just needed the boy slightly further away. "What good fortune," the man remarked slowly.

"One would think, but she has been remarkably difficult to locate."

The man's jaw slackened in surprise. His grip on the boy loosened. "What do you—"

There. Saiph lunged, grabbing the boy and shoving him away as she grasped the man by his throat and pressed him into the wall.

"Why are you helping them?" The man's voice was a rasping gurgle, but Saiph did not ease her grip. She had tried, tried so hard, didn't understand what this rise in hunger was or why it consumed her so, but the blood was seeping into her once more, the heat and fear from the mortal man a temptation she couldn't ignore. All the instincts she had been able to push back at the sight of the young boy in danger, the need to protect swallowing her desire, came flooding back as she leaned in close and tipped the man's neck to the side.

"If wishes were fishes…" she whispered, and the man began to struggle, kicking ineffectively at her legs, free hands lifting to claw at her face and making not even a scratch. As if he could touch her, as if he could truly do any damage. "…you'd all be gutted." She plunged her fangs into his neck, as easy as parting butter, and fed. The first long draw set her nerve endings alight, tingles spreading through her as warmth infused her very soul. She took more, she wasn't sure there would ever be enough. The man's screams began to quiet with each rough tug of her mouth until his blood slowed to a trickle, and a quiet presence approaching set off every inner alert she had. This was her prey. Nobody else's.

Saiph shoved the empty body from her with a blur of motion before sinking into a crouch and hissing at the approaching figure.

Auren raised her hands placatingly. "He was all yours, *seren*." She stopped where she was and lowered her hand to the ground. Saiph followed the motion with suspicious eyes and froze as they found the small boy on the ground where she had shoved him, now coated in a generous layer of his father's blood. His eyes looked too white against the stark red that coated him and his dark hair stuck up at odd angles, like he'd been roused from bed in the middle of this commotion.

Saiph straightened slowly and reached out her own hand to the boy. He stared at it for a second before grasping it firmly and standing with a tug of Saiph's arm.

"Did you kill him?" the boy asked.

"Yes."

He nodded slowly, thoughtfully, as if deciding whether or not she was a monster. "Thank you."

The boy's mother interrupted before she could reply, sweeping the boy into her arms as she knelt on the floor, heedless of the blood of the male soaking into the hem of her cotton dress.

"Kara, Kara," she sobbed, and the boy looked nonplussed as she began to spit on her clothes and wipe away the blood on his face. "Thank you, thank you."

Saiph said nothing, unsure how to respond. She hadn't killed the man for the boy. In the end, that had been entirely about her own gratification. But she had done what she could to ensure he remained safe, out of harm's way. Should she respond in kind? A warm hand wrapped around her bicep and tugged her gently away from the grieving family and the bond, now slumbering again, recognised Auren's proximity.

"She loves him," Saiph said quietly as she watched the mother fawn over the boy.

"Yes," Auren said, watching Saiph's face closely.

"Does your mother love you as keenly as this?" Saiph wasn't sure where the question came from, only that seeing how cherished this child was made her... wistful.

"I don't know. I am an orphan."

Saiph turned to her in surprise. "Who took care of you?"

"Ren and I took care of each other."

She could understand that. She and Vala took care of each other too. "My mother has never said that she loves me."

A beat of hesitation passed before Auren responded. "Some emotions are felt too greatly to express."

Saiph smiled without humour. "Yes, I'm sure that's it."

Auren bit her lip as she watched Saiph's face before turning back to the room and straightening her shoulders. "Raze will be here soon to assist with the clean-up and other arrangements, Morgana," Auren said from beside Saiph and the woman paid them no attention, still frantically scrubbing Kara's face clean as he squirmed to get out of her tight grip.

"Actually," Saiph said, and the boy stopped, as if

entranced by her low, musical voice, "Raze might need some assistance."

Auren frowned but nodded. "I'll take care of it." She looked at Saiph, searching her face as if for answers to questions Saiph could only guess at. "I'll escort you back to your quarters."

"Like I told Raze, I don't need a babysitter."

"The dead body on the floor suggests otherwise."

"I'm only responsible for the one, though I do have questions about the other."

Auren regarded her shrewdly, her lips pursed together as she watched Saiph for a moment in silence. "Fine, let's go."

"Where?"

"Your room."

Saiph sighed, missing her actual room in the Kingdom of Stars, draped with silks and warmth. Though admittedly, she usually cared very little for those kinds of luxuries.

"You said you had questions, Saiph. I'm all too willing to give you answers."

Curiosity peaked and bloodlust slaked, Saiph smirked and followed Auren through the dirt-packed tunnels.

"I am made of questions when it comes to you, witch."

Saiph thought she saw the flicker of a smile on Auren's face before she turned, embracing the darkness fully as they moved further away from the scent of blood and death.

CHAPTER EIGHT
SAIPH

THE LANTERN HAD LONG BURNED OUT WHEN AUREN and Saiph made it back to her room. She could feel the man's blood on her skin still, slightly tacky as it dried, but thankfully her control seemed re-established. She had never felt so lost within herself before. In the Kingdom of Stars, there was no need for these instincts to stir. She did not have a mate there, and it was unusual to bite a casual lover. The mortals remained here, where they couldn't sully the beauty above. More than that, a mortal likely couldn't survive in the Kingdom of Stars. They were like fragile plants needing water and sunlight. The Kingdom of Stars was only darkness and perpetual starlight from the balls of ether that fed their magic—beautiful, but impractical for a human.

"So," Saiph drawled, slowly piecing the parts of herself back together with each breath. "What exactly did I get in the middle of back there?"

Auren shrugged lightly. "It was nothing." Her voice was caught in the shadows, but her face was not, though she likely didn't realise it. Saiph walked to the lantern and relit it quickly.

"Oh? Is it a regular occurrence for men to hold children at knife point here then?"

A tug on her hair, a deep breath, and then Auren said, "No, it's not. But attempts on the queen's life are hardly unexpected."

"And yet, he appeared unsuccessful—unless the heir is a child?"

Auren smirked, a quick twist of her lips that should have looked intimidating with her scar but only made Saiph more curious.

"Does anyone know what your queen looks like?"

A short laugh, echoing in the small room, thrown like the flickering of the flame across the bare walls. "Of course! But when enemies are lurking around every corner"—she gave Saiph a pointed look—"one can't be too careful. I'm a slightly more well-known face as her guard. He must have known to follow me."

"Follow you?" Auren had left her people, her *queen* undefended with her enemy sleeping in their midst. What sort of guard was she? Unless the assassin had been lurking amongst the caves for a while. "You left here by yourself? Recently?" It wasn't unheard of in the Kingdom of Stars, but for a mortal, it was decidedly unusual—they were so vulnerable, hence the large retinues they always travelled in when solitude and shadows were often much more subtle.

"I can take care of myself."

"Mm yes, tell me again about the time you once got kidnapped whilst stalking a star?" Saiph was staring at her incredulously. Who was this woman? Everything about her was a contradiction—she cared for her people, passionately... but she left them here undefended with a deadly enemy in their midst? It was clear Auren strove for calm, but Saiph had seen her close to snapping several times now, the most recent in that room with the piss-poor assassin.

"That was... unfortunate. But unlikely to happen again. Though I appreciate the concern, *seren*, truly. It's sweet." Auren's mouth curved, but the look in her golden eyes was hard, challenging. As though this were a battle she had fought several times and did not wish to rehash—perhaps with her brother?

A laugh rasped out of Saiph's chest. "I do not give two shits about your life, witch, but this bond between us has other ideas. Beyond that fact, if you die with our bargain unfulfilled I don't know what will happen. This is self-preservation, pure and simple."

"And was it self-preservation when you drained that man dry? Remind me again who it is your people believe to be the animals?"

Saiph hissed delicately. "Watch yourself, witch. I saved that boy. I saved that family."

"Did you? Or had other prey just captured your attention more?"

Saiph reared back. "I would never hurt a child. You act as if you know so much about my kind, but if that was true, you would know how sacred children are to us. It's true that I—I lost myself for a moment. Things are different on this plane. There are parts of me waking up that I never needed to control before."

Auren looked at her levelly. It was ridiculous really that this short woman could be staring up at her as if she had all the authority in the world. There was tension in her jaw, and any warmth that usually lingered in her eyes was absent as she said, "You put us all at risk today with your unchecked hunger and rage. You may not be my friend, but I do not count you as an enemy, Saiph."

"You have a very interesting way of showing it."

One of Auren's hands clenched into a fist at her side. "You've been left unsupervised thus far—"

"Oh? Does Raze not count as supervision?"

"I never asked him to watch you. If you thought as much, then you were mistaken."

Saiph ran her eyes across Auren's face, taking in the minute tics of expression—the half twitch of an eyebrow, the softly bitten lip, the tightening of not one, but two fists, and nodded.

"I wanted information from that man, and now he's dead. So I'm going to *politely* ask that you keep your fangs in check."

"Or what?" Saiph stepped forward until she was only a breath away from Auren's face.

"If I feel that you're a danger to anyone here, I will end you."

Surprise flickered through her, there and gone in a moment. "You vastly overestimate your abilities. Besides, I'm not convinced the blood debt would react particularly well to the death of one or both of us before it's been fulfilled."

"I suppose you'll just have to behave yourself and hope that we don't have to find out for sure."

Damned woman. Starlight take her, but Saiph had never met someone so bull-headed. "You will not leave without me again if you're so sloppy as to come back here trailing assassins. Besides, I need to see the stars." Auren's mouth opened and then closed as though considering her words.

"I don't need your help—"

"Auren—"

"—but I will accept it. You'll be leaving here at some point anyway, as soon as Orien sends word. I suppose it might be nice to have company if I need to foray."

That had been... easier than expected. Saiph curled an eyebrow. Auren seemed to have many depths and layers, but Saiph did not think *nice* was in her repertoire.

"Then it's a deal."

Auren nodded, eyes melting back to the liquid gold Sapih had become familiar with as she took a step back from her and then pushed towards the entrance of Saiph's room.

"Oh, and Saiph?"

"Yes, witch?"

"Thank you. For saving the boy."

Had it been a test earlier then? More of her risk analysis? Trying to find out what made Saiph tick? In the end, she said nothing. After all, she hadn't killed the man for them, had she?

CHAPTER NINE
SAIPH

"ARE YOU READY, *SEREN?*" AUREN ASKED HER THE NEXT day, breezing through her door as if she owned the place. Which she may well, Saiph mused. She had gone searching for the heir again last night and had found nothing but quiet. The mortals were scarce, spending time with their families in light of the recent death of one of their own, and the tunnels had been deserted.

"For what?" Saiph responded, ignoring the term of endearment that Auren used so liberally around her. Or was it a joke at her expense? All of Saiph's people were the same, degrees of light or dark. There was no sunlight in the kingdom and Saiph's skin showed evidence of that fact, a pale so delicate she glowed with the starlight she had absorbed. But silver? Saiph had yet to puzzle out the nickname.

"For a tour, of course. You've been hunting us for

so long—how can I not show you what you've been missing?"

Despite herself, excitement shot through Saiph as it always did when she was on a hunt. Though, admittedly, her latest was not going quite to plan. Her mother had bade her a simple task: *find the false heir, kill the false heir.* It wasn't over yet though. Auren was the protector of the queen; she could use that. Find the queen's weaknesses, the weaknesses of the rebels and their stronghold, and destroy them from the inside.

A loud laugh cut through the silence Saiph hadn't noticed descend. "Oh, *seren*, you were not blessed with a poker face. The look of wild glee that came over you just then was extraordinary to behold." A burn of something like embarrassment flooded through her, momentarily stealing her tongue, but Auren simply laughed again, her eyes like brown fire as they ran across Saiph's skin. "I didn't expect you to be so…"

"So?"

"Savage." Auren grinned. "I can't say I dislike it. I suppose you live up to the rumours."

"You'd heard of me?" Auren seemed to have shed her solemn demeanour of the night before. In fact, she seemed *warm*—that, of course, immediately made her suspicious. Which face of Auren's was true?

"Who hasn't heard of the heir to the Kingdom of Stars?" Auren said with a smirk laced in mystery as she strode purposefully past Saiph to the door. "Coming?"

Saiph said nothing, merely followed her out the door and into the mess undoubtedly waiting beyond.

Auren moved confidently through the dirt-packed tunnels, illuminated once more by soft lantern light every few feet.

Random humans nodded to Auren as they passed, casting Saiph only brief and curious glances. No doubt they had all heard of yesterday's bloody countenance and of her part in it. She could hear them murmuring to one another about the wake, the final rites for the deceased father, and Saiph wondered briefly what might have become of the assassin's drained body.

One young child gazed openly at her as they passed, and Saiph allowed a small chuckle to climb free from her chest as the child's eyes widened, tugging on the sleeve of the woman accompanying them urgently. "Mama, mama, that lady has *fangs!*" The young woman shot Saiph a look of apology, which was in itself surprising. "Can I have fangs too, Mama?"

"No, sweet. Now hush—"

Their conversation faded away as Saiph and Auren rounded a corner to find a dead end. She raised a brow lazily. Was this Auren's attempt at a trap? If so, she was disappointed.

"Where are we?" Saiph asked, voice pitched low. Auren shivered as Saiph's breath stirred the fine hairs on the back of her neck. Her bloodlust seemed to have been slaked last night, but Auren pushed buttons Saiph hadn't known she had and the chance to taunt, to tease, was too hard to pass up.

"You'll see," Auren said, sweeping back a dark curtain that would have been impossible to notice unless you knew it was there. In the low light, the flaps of material fluttered ominously and Saiph's breath sped up. Sometimes a trap was as good as a seduction. The battle of cunning and wits, the domination of strength and surrender…

Auren swept inside without a backward glance, and Saiph touched her tongue to an aching fang as she followed swiftly. The room was cast in orange, several nests of flames flickering in recesses built into the walls, filling the room with a surprising heat. The floor was separated into a large square, a rudimentary fighting ring, and Saiph could taste the tang of old sweat and anger on her tongue like bitter lemon, begging for a bite. She'd never had to worry about self-control before, had never had any impulses wild enough to worry. But this could be pushing her beyond her limits.

"I don't want to spar," Saiph rasped around her fangs and suddenly dry throat.

"Well, I do," Auren said, turning to face her with a smile made wicked by the scar that cleaved her bottom lip. She was like a flame, bronzed and flickering in time with the fire, and Saiph felt herself sway towards the ring, almost feeling the first taste of Auren's blood on her tongue.

No. The blood debt surely would not allow it. It could too easily lead to Auren's death, though Saiph was sure she would at least try to hold her own.

"I do not draw my swords lightly," Saiph responded, "and I have no need for hand-to-hand combat. Not with you."

"Is that so?" Auren murmured softly before stepping a gentle foot forward. The sound of scraping dirt dragged across Saiph's senses like a groan, everything heightened, all on extreme. Faster than Auren could blink, Saiph flashed forward and behind her, letting her mouth lower to an inch above her sweet-smelling skin and blowing softly.

"Yes," Saiph breathed. "I could end you between heartbeats, and you would beg for more."

She could feel Auren's consideration by the slight tension in her neck and shoulders before she nodded.

"Then swords it will be."

Saiph's mouth snapped open in protest but found a dagger at her heart before she could blink.

"I suggest you ready yourself."

Saiph fingered the hilts of *Vidi* and *Iudi* and moved several paces back, as was customary. Auren faced her once more, a smile flashing across her face when she found Saiph's hands resting on her weapons. Then her hand shot out blindingly fast as she threw her dagger.

"Impressive," Saiph said as she effortlessly caught the sharp blade in mid-air with one hand just as it brushed her chest, a flare of surprise flashing through her as she recognised it as star-spun steel. "You would have hit my heart."

"I knew you would catch it."

Saiph prowled slowly forward and heard Auren's breath stutter before resuming its slow, even pace. So she did make her nervous after all. Saiph cleaned the blood from her hand off of Auren's blade, running her tongue down and over the sharp point before handing it back, hilt first.

"What do they mean?" Auren asked, not even reaching for the simple blade, now shining anew. Saiph glanced behind her to see where her attention was.

"The blades?"

"Yes. I know a great deal of your customs through research, but I never learned your tongue. Or, not more than the odd word here and there, anyway."

Saiph considered her for a moment, the way the heat from the lanterns seemed to have been absorbed into her skin and was now shimmering in the space between them. The flat curiosity in her deep eyes, like the need for this knowledge was deeper than Saiph could imagine, a wall built safely around it. She pulled *Vidi* from its sheath, and the blade sang like a sigh as it cut through the air to plant into the ground between them.

"To see, to protect. It is a gentler magic than its twin blade, *Iudi.* Judge. Slayer. Justice."

"These are qualities that are important to you?" Auren's head tilted to the side, analysing Saiph for her answer and she let a small smirk flirt with the edges of her lips. Saiph's eyes flickered to the long arc of the throat Auren had revealed, saw the pulse fluttering there, and blinked, tamping down on the need that arose. Something about these hot-blooded mortals was amping up every instinct Saiph had never needed to fight. It was... uncomfortable.

"I did not name them. They found me. They are

ancient blades and necessary balances. One to protect and one to fight. It is said that when used together, they are nearly unstoppable."

"Strange, isn't it, how love is often thought of as weakness by your kind, but wielding it is your greatest strength."

Saiph let a throaty laugh tear from her and Auren blinked, surprised. "You do not know me. Nor my kind. I have never drawn both blades, and I likely never will. What could I possibly have to protect?"

"Perhaps you will find out," Auren said with an odd tilt to her chin, stepping closer into the finite space between them. "You said they are nearly unstoppable. What could have more power?"

"*Quaesitum*," Saiph said, voice soft as though saying the word aloud may draw its attention, despite that her mother could no more see them in that moment than peer through a solid wall. "Conqueror." For there were some powers greater than even her own. Auren nodded thoughtfully, and the too-small gap between them became electric.

"I think you may surprise yourself yet, *seren*." Auren's full mouth was tantalisingly close and Saiph wasn't sure which disturbed her more, the urge to claim it or to drink from it. She tore herself away. It had to be the bond and this strange new bloodlust. Being on the mortal plane had changed her in ways she couldn't have prepared for.

Saiph took another step back. This could not happen, rampant instincts or no. Auren was off-limits. Her mother would have her head if she stooped so low as to take a mortal. It had been expressly forbidden by law once her mother came into power. Though admittedly, this was to prevent any potential off-shoots such a pairing could provide, and this definitely wouldn't be an issue for her and Auren.

No. Absolutely not. She wasn't sure what Auren's game was, but this... temptation had to be part of it. But why?

A draft flickered through the room, and Saiph let the cool kiss of her blade press to a throat before she processed moving. Raze fixed his cold eyes on hers as the curtain to the sparring room fell closed once more and then ignored her, looking instead to Auren.

"Your brother sent word of more disappearances down in Sommer. You can leave by next light." Raze did not seem to mind the slow trickle of blood that stirred as his throat moved, and Saiph pulled back as Auren began to move forward.

"Good. I think we were done here anyway."

"I thought you wanted to spar?" Saiph could have cursed her foolhardy tongue for letting the words slip free.

"Is that not what we were doing, *seren?*" Auren answered silkily, her back to Saiph but head tilted slightly to the side, the brown in her hair melting to gold as she swept from the room once more. Raze sighed in front of her and Saiph nearly started, having forgotten he was there.

"This way... Highness." He said it like it was a foreign word, unused to the taste of it on his tongue.

Saiph shook free of her stupor and brushed a smirk across her face. "I'll tell you the same thing I told Orien. Next time, you should be on your knees."

Raze huffed a quiet laugh and Saiph smirked wider, finding the steady man comforting in a way she had never experienced before in a male. There were, of course, all genders in the Kingdom of Stars, but generally they were paid little attention to. Your power meant more than gender or beauty ever could. In fact, there were many who subscribed to no gender at all.

"I'll be sure to remember that next time. My queen wouldn't want me to offend the foreign dignitaries."

"How's your wrist?"

Raze blinked in surprise, as if not expecting her to care—but it was only polite to inquire about an injury, especially one she had caused.

Raze smiled and held up his arm for her to see, clenching his fist experimentally. "Good as new."

Saiph raised her eyebrows. "You have a healer here?"

A light shrug was his only answer, but he gestured her towards the door with a courtly bow and flourished with the same arm, and Saiph grinned, curiouser and curiouser.

A shout cut through the air, and Raze tensed beside her. They shared a quick glance before hurrying through the curtain after Auren.

"Witch?" Saiph called, anger a slow fizz in her

veins. If she had gone out again... dragged another assassin back after assuring Saiph she could accompany her next time—

Raze and Saiph found Auren just around the bend, her hand placed comfortingly on the same mother Saiph had met the night prior.

"He can't have gone far, Morgana. We'll find him," Auren said soothingly. She exuded that same dark calm she had pushed onto Saiph when she had just arrived. Watching it from the outside sent a chill down her spine, but she could not quite place why.

"What if another got in and took him?" Morgana was a mess. Her hands ran repeatedly through her hair, tugging at the greying strands as if standing still was too much for her to take.

"We ran a full search last night. He was the only one who got through. He's probably just wandered off. You know these tunnels are extensive. We'll find him."

Saiph closed her eyes and inhaled deeply. Morgana began to mutter, and Saiph sensed Auren drawing closer to the woman and knew she was about to speak, heard the faint sound of her lips parting before Saiph snapped, "Quiet."

A tension fell over them, and she could feel eyes pressing in on her. She ignored them and sent her senses out, searching. Usually, she kept a tight leash on her senses, not wanting to overwhelm herself with a million tastes, sounds, and smells. But sometimes... a fluttering heartbeat sounded out, the saltiness of tears tanged on her tongue, and a slight snuffle sounded as close by as if it were right next to her ear. Saiph ran, letting the sound guide her as it vibrated off the walls, cascading against her skin until her teeth clenched with the rise of emotion she could feel tugging at her, drawing her nearer. Despair, guilt.

She found him huddled in a crevice a few breaths later. How his small body had wriggled in there, Saiph couldn't imagine. It was dark, but she could see him just fine. He blinked blearily, tears trembling on his lashes as he searched the darkness, as if stirred by the faint breeze of Saiph's movement. This one was smart, good instincts. Most mortals didn't realise something lurked in the dark until it was far too late.

She let some of her light, carefully locked away beneath her glamour, begin to leak free from her pores and held her hand out, palm up, for the child. His eyes went wide as they took her in.

"Come, child. Your mother is frantic."

The boy, Kara, she dimly recalled, hesitated before shaking his head, and she released a small sigh as she crouched down a little further to gaze steadily into his eyes. "Why are you hiding, *stellula*?"

Kara resumed his hiccupping sobs. "I helped the man."

Saiph considered him briefly. What would be best here? She was not a parent and knew even less about human children than she did her own kind. "The assassin, you mean?"

Kara nodded, The tears pouring free from his eyes were washing away the dirt scrubbed onto his cheeks, no doubt attained from his climb into this nook. "I found him in the tunnels. He said he had an important message for the queen, so I took him to my papa."

Saiph nodded slowly. "He would have found his way eventually, *stellula*. If not you, then it doubtless would have been someone else. It was not your job to protect the queen or the tunnels."

Kara jerked as if hit with a bolt of lightning. He glared at her fiercely, and she heard his little heart beat harder as he shook. "*No*. We are together. We fight and we bleed together. We love and we die for the queen and kingdom."

Such bold words for one so young, and Saiph raised her hands in placation and smiled slightly as he became distracted by her glowing skin. "So perhaps it was your job, little one. But the Fates are cruel and not often dissuaded. It is pointless to worry about what might or could have been."

His face buried in his hands, Kara let out a cry that seemed driven from his very soul and something in Saiph felt like it withered in response. How many more young felt pain like this in this world? How many were because of her throne? Saiph moved without thinking, tugging the boy out of the crevice and into her arms as she slid to the dirt floor with him clasped tightly to her. She knew now what she should have said all along.

"I'm sorry for your papa, *stellula*. He is at peace among the stardust now. You were right to take the man to him. What if someone else had found him and the assassin had hurt them? Or what if he found his way to your queen instead? You are brave, and I am certain your papa would be proud."

Kara peered up at her from below Saiph's chin, eyes watery but hopeful. "They want me to say goodbye to him, but I don't know how to stand at his side when I know I caused his death."

Saiph raised a brow. "Did you wield the blade?"

"Well, no—"

"Then let your soul rest easy knowing your papa's death was avenged. You must take this sad but necessary lesson and remember it always. People are not always as they seem."

Kara looked up at her for a few more moments before settling down with his head curled against her neck and his arms around her middle. She heard his breathing slow and felt her own tension drain away. He was asleep.

CHAPTER TEN
SAIPH

FEET SCUFFED LIGHTLY AGAINST THE DIRT FLOOR AND jolted Saiph awake. She blinked around in confusion. Her skin had dimmed, her starlight locked back up inside tightly, and a furnace was pressed tightly to her chest. She glanced down and found Kara, still deeply asleep, and Saiph realised with a guilty jolt that she must have succumbed too. His mother was likely out of her mind by now. It was the first decent rest Saiph had managed since being underground though, so she couldn't bring herself to feel *too* sorry. More noise emerged from the corridor and lantern light illuminated the dirt walls, painting them orange as Auren, Morgana, and two other men rounded the corner and stopped short. One of the men, a young mortal with pale skin and deep-set eyes, opened his mouth, and Saiph hissed quietly, pressing a finger to her lips and glancing meaningfully down at Kara. Auren looked to be suppressing some sort of emotion.

Saiph caught the flare of triumph in her eyes and felt unease skitter across her skin.

Morgana was not to be deterred though and quickly leapt forward with a sprightliness that surprised Saiph. She let a flare of warmth flit through Kara and he woke slowly, patting a small hand against Saiph's face as his mother pulled him into her arms. Her blue eyes were like the ocean, spilling salt water and relief into the air, and Saiph became uncomfortably aware of the dryness of her throat, of the hunger slinking through her bones. She stood in one fluid motion, needing to escape the oppressing call of the blood thrumming through the mortal's veins. One of the mortal men lightly gasped as she faced the lantern light, and she knew what they likely saw, eyes dark as pitch, the fangs that she had hidden for Kara's sake now lowered and gleaming in the light.

"Y-your Highness?" a small voice called, and Saiph came back to herself slightly, turning to look at the small creature as reason began to seep into her again. Saiph closed her mouth, hiding her fangs away as she gave a close-lipped smile to Kara.

"Come now, *stellula*, I think we are past such formalities."

Kara let a tremulous smile pass across his mouth before he fell back into nervousness. "Saiph, will you come with me to see my papa?"

She blinked back her surprise. These mortals crawled beneath your skin and carved their way into your hearts. But, she supposed, the damage was done

—she would likely flay anyone who attempted to harm the young boy and smile all the while.

Auren spoke before Saiph could. "Actually, Kara, Saiph and I need to make haste to Sommer."

Saiph raised an eyebrow. "Surely we have time —"

Auren's face remained impassive. "We would have, if you hadn't decided to sleep for six hours."

Six hours? No wonder she felt stiff. How had it taken them so long to find them? These tunnels must have been more extensive than Saiph realised. She'd barely focused on them as she'd run to find Kara, only listening out for his heart and the scent of his quiet tears.

Releasing a heavy sigh, Saiph turned her back to Auren and the men, sinking down to her knees before Kara. "I'm sorry, *stellula*, I have to go. Remember what I said." She made to stand and then hesitated. The surge of protectiveness she felt for this small mortal was not something she had ever experienced before and, for a second, it took her breath. "If you need me, summon me and I will come." Without warning, Saiph sliced into her hand with her fangs, offering her blood to the old magick, something no star had attempted to call on for starlight knew how long. Her blood solidified in her hand as her sacrifice was accepted, and she cast a little of her own starlight into it for good measure before handing the faintly glowing blood crystal to the boy. "Just squeeze it and think of me. It will only work once," she warned him, and he gave a solemn nod. His warm brown eyes held hers for a moment before he coiled forward and sprung at her. Her muscles stiffened in surprise, but she held perfectly still as he wrapped his arms around her and squeezed tightly before letting go and following his mother down the path of the tunnels to where his papa's body awaited.

Saiph remained on her knees a moment longer before standing in a blur that had one of the mortal men skittering back a step. He blew out a harsh breath that washed over Saiph, hitting her with the temptation to take, to feed, and her eyes slid shut as she attempted to reign her instincts in.

"I think it might be best for you to leave now, Aven. We ought not to be gone for too long, but remember what I said all the same."

Aven, the male who had skittered away from her like a spooked bug, nodded and caught a hold of the other man, tugging him away the way they'd come.

"Come, *seren*, we need to get you out of here before you decide to snack on one of the queen's subjects."

"Surely she won't notice just a small bite?" Saiph purred, letting her tongue sweep longingly across her bottom lip and watching Auren's eyes follow the movement with a satisfaction that should have troubled her.

"I'm certain she would notice," Auren said with a light clear of her throat and a small quirk of her lips betraying her amusement. "Come, I've already packed everything we may need and have a cloak readied for you too."

Saiph accepted it with a curt nod. It was a deep

blue and surprisingly soft. It wasn't often the stars felt the cold, not when they burned with their own fire, but it was a nice gesture all the same. Besides, the heavy hood would help disguise her *otherness* at least a little. There was only so much a glamour could do.

Auren eyed the supple, stretchy material of Saiph's trousers and the equally flexible top that covered most of her skin. "You'll stand-out in those clothes. Do you want to borrow some leathers?"

Saiph grimaced. She'd rather stand-out than drape herself in the hardened skin of an animal. Her clothes were supple but strong, allowing her full flexibility when fighting—besides, there weren't many human weapons that could cause her much damage anyway. Her skin was impervious to most human blades. Though, Auren was proving to be the exception, and Saiph wondered briefly how she might fare against a blade of magic tempered with Auren's gold.

Apparently reading her disgust from her face, Auren rolled her eyes and began to lead them deeper into the tunnel, away from the direction the men had taken. Saiph growled lightly in annoyance but perked up at the realisation that they would soon be out from the tunnels, breathing fresh air, taking countenance with the night sky.

Auren smiled, as if sensing Saiph's excitement, and hitched the leather bag she was holding higher onto her shoulder beneath her own cloak. Saiph had assumed they were deep within the mountains that bypassed the largest river nearby. She had never bothered learning the town name, not when it had barely passed for any sort of community. Though, if Orien and Auren were to be believed, the fault lay with the Kingdom of Stars for that. But if they were in the mountains, then that meant the likeliest exit would be—

Auren led them up a sharp incline that would have had any mortal panting, but Auren's heart remained steady and not a drop of sweat graced her face. She reached the top and pushed outward on a small, jutting piece of rock, smirking as the seemingly dead end rolled away with a groan. Cool air brushed Saiph's face and she took in a greedy breath, ready to rush out of the cave network until she glimpsed what lay beyond. Trees, dark firs as far as she could see, and a darkness so penetrating that even the rising dawn didn't touch their tops.

It was the Forest, a place so riddled with old magick that even the stars couldn't counter it. She hadn't remembered the old stories when she'd first arrived on the mortal plane, simply sensing something *other* about the trees. No wonder the rebels had been living in the caves undetected for so long. They were practically within the Forest itself. It was said that the old magick could cloak the sight of the stars, and it looked like the rumours held some truth as Saiph had seen nothing of the rebel encampment before she had come to this plane and neither had her mother. Instead, she had been forced to hunt down rebels in the open with the hope that they could lead her here. What would happen if she were to enter? Would the Forest swallow her whole like it would any starlight that was within its borders? What price had the rebels paid to safely lodge within its shadow?

Her hunger was quelled by the rising tide of fear that clouded her vision. She turned to Auren incredulously. "You expect me to travel through there?"

Auren blinked at her innocently, her face perfectly blank as though carved from the mountains itself in its terrible beauty. "Don't tell me you're scared of some trees, *seren?* What happened to you *insisting* to accompany me next time I left?"

"Those," Saiph said with a sharp jab of her finger in the direction of the Forest, "are no mere trees. There must be a way around them."

"Possibly," Auren said with a quick nod while she examined her fingernails, "but we won't be going that way. It takes too long, and this is safest." Auren didn't wait for any more protests as she began walking down a slope that led to the dense foliage. Saiph cursed but followed, her heart beating strangely loud in her ears.

"Safest for you, maybe. I'm not comfortable with this."

A trace of a smirk ghosted across Auren's face, and her hips swayed a little more the closer they got to the edge of the Forest. "Yes, I can't imagine you would be."

Saiph muttered unpleasantries under her breath, and the witch's smirk only grew as Saiph's curses became more inventive the closer they got to the darkness. A tendril reached out, wrapping itself around Auren as if in welcome, like she was a familiar traveller saying hello to an old friend. Another tendril reached out and brushed against Saiph's magic, and she couldn't help the catch in her breath as the old magick of the Forest pulled away her glamour. Starlight blazed whitely against the deep trees, and they swallowed it whole as though it were a delicacy they'd not had in a long while.

"Auren, I really don't think—"

"Hush, *stellula*. All will be fine. You are with me."

It was true that the Forest seemed to like Auren, rustling its leaves in welcome, letting the small patches of grass climb her legs and curling affectionately around her calves.

Saiph snorted at her choice of nickname. "I may be a star, but I'm certainly not little."

Auren grinned and the darkness seemed to ripple in response, like a playful puppy eager to please as they moved further amongst the trees. "It was an interesting choice of words for him."

"You disapprove?"

"No, it was… nice."

Nice. Saiph didn't think anybody had ever described her as such. Wrathful, savage, even down-right monstrous, but never *nice*.

"Yes, well, even the stars value the young."

Auren looked at her in surprise. "Kara is nine years old."

Saiph shrugged, was that old for a mortal child? The starlight babies matured much slower than a regular mortal on account of their immortality. Nine years old seemed like nothing. Of course, by the time Saiph was eleven she had already learned to wield a sword. Her mother, the true queen, was not particularly maternal. Sometimes she wondered what life would have been like without Vala, her twin. They had given each other the love Queen Fallon could likely never give. Knowing what she now did, Saiph wondered if perhaps she and Auren were more alike than she'd initially thought. Saiph felt like she knew Auren on a soul-to-soul level, something within her calling to Saiph like a moth to a flame and just as likely to be burned. Yet, she knew surprisingly little about her, and Orien too, she supposed. Saiph drew her mind away from thoughts of Auren and back to where they should be. The false queen.

"Who is protecting the heir in your absence?"

Auren's heart thudded unevenly, and Saiph raised a brow. Why should these words cause such alarm?

"Aven and Raze. Aven is—"

Saiph smirked as she cast her mind back to the mortal man who had stumbled away from her in fright. "I remember."

Auren rolled her eyes. "You're so predictably violent."

Saiph felt a stab of irritation that seemed to draw the attention of the lingering dark and worked quickly to wash it away. "I don't think violence is predictable. It's *consistent.*"

Auren hummed quietly and tree branches bowed down as she walked below them, as if trying to get impossibly closer. "And offering summoning crystals that bind you by blood, are those consistent for you too?"

"Jealous, witch? I would have thought our blood debt would be more than enough to fulfil all the *aches* you have for me." Saiph wasn't sure where the taunting words had come from, but she was certain that Auren liked them.

"Not jealous, no. Merely surprised at how eager you are to further entangle yourself with us lowly mortals. Your mother must be more progressive than I realised."

A low growl snuck out of Saiph's throat and there was a pause in the dark, like it had finally had its attention drawn away from Auren long enough to truly notice what lurked beneath Saiph's skin. She pushed her anger down deeply, not wanting to provoke the Forest, and chanced a glance up through the trees and fought back a shudder. Not a single ray of light broke through the canopy of trees and midnight. Saiph knew that if it were the middle of the night, she would not be able to see the stars. If the Forest decided to claim her for itself, she would never be found in this place where even the stars could not *see*.

"Progressive is perhaps not quite the word I would use to describe Queen Fallon."

Auren's smile turned ice cold. "I can't imagine why," she said dryly. "Come, we still have a ways to walk yet, and I want to be at Somnia before full sun-break. The Forest will help us out where it can."

"It can do that?"

"I find there is very little the darkness won't do for me."

"What are we looking for, exactly?"

Auren glanced at her quickly before re-training her gaze to the trees ahead of them. How she had any sense of where they walked, Saiph didn't know.

"My brother sent word of a large batch of disappearances in Sommer, that's our southern counterparts."

"Yes." Saiph rolled her eyes. "I am somewhat familiar with the geography of your realm."

Auren shrugged lightly. "Just being thorough, *seren*, starlight knows what they teach you up there."

She sniffed, irritated. "Teach *us*? Do you even have schools here for your young? Libraries?"

The footfalls at her side ceased and the darkness seemed to swell as it pulsed like a living creature around Auren, her amber eyes glowing in the dark that threatened to consume them before it eased. Saiph was relieved. It was unwise to wield such magic in the Forest. Who knew what manner of creature may come looking for its source.

"We did once," Auren said softly, and Saiph stiffened. "We had libraries and schools and museums, all destroyed. You can thank your mother for that."

"My mother? You realise it was the mortals who slayed your king and queen and ruined the peace they had fought so hard for?"

"Tell me, when your mother feeds you such lies, do you ever question them?" Auren's mouth was a hard line, unforgiving as she waved the darkness away from her and continued on, carving her path through the trees and leaving Saiph to begrudgingly follow. "Such an interesting account of events Queen Fallon touts, almost as if she was there for the creation of Somnium itself."

Saiph inhaled a sharp breath as her head whipped towards Auren. "That name is forbidden and long forgotten. It is treason to speak it. What do you know of it?"

A roll of Auren's eyes met Saiph's words. "As if I care for treasonous words in the face of a traitor queen. I know a great many things, Saiph. It is very clear to me that you do not."

Saiph snapped her teeth, not appreciating Auren's tone or condescending words, and the dark of the Forest seemed to shiver around her. Not that she needed the warning. The bond handled that just fine, zipping a shock up her spine before Saiph could take so much as a step in the witch's direction.

"My mother is no traitor," she settled for snarling and Auren laughed, the sound twirling amongst the leaves as they walked endlessly.

"You said it to me yourself. *Quaesitum*. Your queen

stole my queen's throne through blood and deception. If you believe anything else you are a fool."

"You speak as if you were there, *witch*. Perhaps you should consider tightening your lips on subjects where you are misinformed before I silence your tongue permanently."

Auren stopped ahead of her and turned, smirking at Saiph like she was glad to have gotten the rise out of her. "Good luck with that, *stellula*. You would be signing away your own death if you tried—I wonder how your sweet mother would feel about that?"

Saiph scowled, refusing to answer as she instead continued walking ahead, only to freeze a moment later at the sight of glowing eyes peering through the darkness before them.

Auren grabbed her arm, and Saiph frowned down at the contact as Auren tugged them quickly away from the path of the monster and onto another, barely discernible, trail. The witch was familiar with these woods, and they with her. It was a discomfiting thought that this mortal, who shone with the power of the dark gods themselves, could look into the dark and be unafraid of what might look back.

CHAPTER ELEVEN
ORIEN

ORIEN KNOCKED BACK THE LAST OF HIS ALE WITH A grimace. Eloria was possibly the closest functioning town to the caves, but it had a piss-poor excuse for booze. It currently sat as the capital of Viridis after most of the towns in the north had fallen to disarray. The north had fared much worse than Sommer, and its capital Somnia, and was nothing compared to the infamous market of the south. That was where the *really* good alcohol could be found, plus a myriad of other items like spices, fabrics, meats... Some things available there were more pleasant than others.

Valentina grinned at him from across the bar, likely flirting her way into another free drink. She was beautiful. There was no denying nor avoiding it. She knew it and was unafraid to wield it where necessary. It wasn't even vanity, just sheer truth. Three fingers pressed to a chest, a laugh with her head tipped back to show the creamy expanse of throat leading to an impressive decolletage that Orien himself had admired several times that evening. That was all it took, a laugh and a touch, and Valentina was stalking back across the room to his side, a shot of whiskey warm on her breath. Even when they'd first met, with her covered in the dirt and dust that seemed to pervade the hot air in Somnia, she had been breathtaking.

"Don't look so put out, Ren. You know I don't pay for my own drinks if I can help it." Her red lips were pursed in a pout, but Valentina's heavy-lashed eyes danced with amusement, baiting him. He bit.

"And what of me? I would buy you all the drinks you could ever want."

"Nice of you to admit that you're trying to get me drunk, if only the rest of these gentlemen would be so forthright!" she called loudly and laughter rang out, with more than one appreciative leer finding her through the crowd near the bar.

Orien rolled his eyes. It was always the same. Valentina dared him to come a little closer. He moved. She ran. His eyes drifted vaguely down to her throat, where her pulse beat steady half-hidden in the thick curtain of her dark curly hair. Her throat cleared in gentle reprimand, and Orien glanced up to find her equally dark eyes batting at him. He'd known since the moment her blood had spilled during a brawl that she was his mate, chosen for him by the Fates who, as everyone knew, had a cruel sense of humour. Not everyone knew straight away, but Orien's senses were sharper than most. He had no idea if it was common to mate with a human or if the Fates were just being particularly difficult, either way, his heart belonged to her.

Valentina loved him, of this, Orien was certain, but she didn't trust him—or rather, his nature. And so their bond went unfulfilled, until the day she would finally let his fangs sink deep. He shook off the provocative thought. The truth was that he understood her reluctance. The stars were not to be trusted and, despite her love and his character, he couldn't change his blood and the way that it changed him—the fangs, his need for blood to keep his magick replenished, the heightened senses... He was not mortal, only half, and he could only hope that in time, Valentina would be able to get past it.

"You were easy to find this time, love."

Valentina offered a secretive smile that coyly curled the corners of her mouth. "Perhaps I didn't run quite so far after our last encounter."

Orien snorted, *encounter*. It was an interesting way for her to describe the thorough seduction she had unravelled for him, only to leave him naked, tied to a bed in a cheap tavern down in Sommer while she laughed her way out the door. He'd lost his favourite dagger that night. It was one Auren had thieved for him when they were sixteen, a silver blade that'd she'd infused with her fire and a blue gem inlaid into the hilt. He'd spotted it strapped to Valentina's thigh when her full skirts had parted at the edges as she had perched on the bar earlier to swindle a shot out of another man.

Orien let a smile full of promise linger on his lips as he waved to the barkeep for another beer. He would have his dagger back before the night drew to a close. Though, unlike so many others, he wouldn't be underestimating his mate. On the surface, Valentina was a gorgeous face, a well-to-do woman, even. It was only when you looked a little closer that you could see the slits in her woollen skirts for easy dagger access— only when you touched her palm that you could feel the rough calluses that betrayed her expertise with a blade and the subtle strength that indicated she knew how to wield it. More than anything, Valentina knew how to wield *him*.

They had been playing this game for longer than he could remember, the Fates pulling them in and Valentina pushing them out. She was human. Undeniably and unbearably so, but she was his regardless. The song of his soul—*anima lux,* his soul light. So, he continued to chase, because he was already hers.

"Your sister has the biggest balls of anyone I've ever met to be attempting this."

Orien laughed and looked up at Valentina through his lashes. "Come now, love, we both know that's not true. You did tie me to a bed, after all." A faint flush of pink spread across Valentina's cheeks, there one minute and gone the next, and he had to bite back his grin of triumph. "Well, you know Auren. Once she has her mind set on something, starlight save us all from getting in her way."

"I know, but a star? The heir to the throne, no less! She's going to get herself killed. Plus, I don't know how she can stand to be near one of *them*." She set her jaw, but her gaze softened when she saw the hurt flit briefly across his face. "Oh, Ren, I'm sorry. You know it's not the same."

He nodded stiffly but couldn't stop seeing the contempt on her face in his head. Was it really all that different? Saiph was arrogant and naive, but he didn't truly think her a monster. How could he when he was just like her? Perhaps that's why she unnerved him so, aside from the danger he felt his sister was flirting with, of course.

Nevertheless, he didn't feel it was worth risking all they had accomplished for Auren's harebrained plan to seduce the heir and reclaim what was rightfully hers. Saiph was too blinded by loyalty to her mother to be swayed by his sister's charms.

"Nothing short of love or a soul bound would be enough to get Saiph on our side."

Valentina grinned devilishly. "I suppose we best hope Auren is an excellent lay."

Orien grimaced and drained the fresh beer the barkeep had brought over. "That's really no way to speak about your queen."

She laughed and pushed away from their rough-hewn wooden table, heedless of splinters. "I need another drink."

He flipped her a silver coin. "If we're going to talk about my sister fucking the heir to the throne, then you best make it two."

Another tinkling laugh was her only response as she sashayed back to the bar and returned a few minutes later with far more than the two drinks on a tray. She threw him a wink, and he sighed in return before plucking one of the small tin whiskey tumblers from the tray and swallowing the drink in one gulp.

"What have you heard on the wind so far, little bird?"

Valentina slid smoothly onto the wooden stool across from him, her body tensing slightly as she focused on who may be listening, on what info she needed to shroud. While she undoubtedly enjoyed the free drinks and appreciative looks, Valentina's true talent was information. It was amazing what people let slip to a pretty face.

Her face darkening, she leaned in close and he couldn't avoid breathing in the sweet violet, dark scent of her. "It's bad, Orien. More people are going missing every day, all of them magick users."

"What could they hope to gain from taking them?"

"I don't know, but they're doing it in the name of the queen."

"Auren would never condone this."

Valentina sighed, massaging her brow before letting her hand drop back down to the table a hairsbreadth from his. "I know. I'll keep digging, but if anyone knows anything, they're not talking."

THE LINGERING DARK

A grim smile took over his face. "You just focus on finding someone. I'll worry about getting them to talk."

Valentina nodded vaguely, picking up and downing another shot of whiskey.

"Easy tiger, I'd prefer not to have to carry you to bed."

Her mouth twitched, but her eyes were heated when they met his. "No, you'd prefer I crawled."

A dart of desire shot through him. He couldn't deny her words spoke a sort of wicked pleasure into him.

"What I *want* is for you to come back to the caves with me."

"You know I can't do that."

Orien gave a small sigh, because he did know. Valentina wasn't meant for hiding in the dark. "Then I suppose you'll have to carry on as our eyes and ears."

"And what lovely eyes and ears they are too," Valentina teased, licking a drop of whiskey off of the side of her tin cup and swallowing.

"Yes," Orien said in somewhat of a daze, following the movement of her throat before shaking himself free and focusing back on the information he needed. "How are they identifying the magick users? Maybe if we find out the how…"

"We can discover the why." Valentina nodded, a small frown puckering her face, and Orien ached to smooth away the lines on her forehead. "I'll see what I can find out. If I had someone to hand over, then maybe more ears might turn my way."

Orien smiled slowly, a plan beginning to form in his head. "Yes. See who you can turn your way, and then when the time comes for the hand-over..."

"We'll be waiting." Valentina smirked, and their gazes caught as sparks seemed to eat up the space between them. "Have you got it under control?"

His heart raced so quickly he was sure she must have been able to see it through the cotton material of his white shirt. He knew what she was asking, what she wanted, but he had to be honest.

"It's hard to keep it in check with you." The urge to claim, to mark, to ensure she was only his was overwhelming when they were together, but he'd promised her he wouldn't bite. Not until she was ready. "Grant me a moment?"

Some of the heat cooled from her expression, but she nodded. She needed this, needed *him*. It had been too long—for the both of them.

Orien stood and made his way to a door on the far side of the tavern. In the low light, he watched another male stand and make his way to the bathroom. *Perfect.* The man was stocky, but his strength would be nothing in comparison to Orien's. He didn't bother checking behind him as he pushed through the door and made his way down the steps that waited. Orien made his move as soon as the man rounded the corner of the final step, darting down faster than the human eye could track, pressing him against the wall and sinking his fangs in deep. The man groaned, and Orien couldn't stop the rumble of pleasure from escaping his own chest as the hot blood coated his tongue and eased the hunger in his bones. It wasn't as good as the blood of a magick user—they replenished him much faster—but blood was blood, and the small spark of life within all humans would be enough to sustain him for now.

He wouldn't kill him. He had better control than that, but he did need to leave him somewhere until he recovered. Orien slid his tongue over the small puncture wounds and watched with satisfaction as they healed over. He hid his fangs away and helped the man to the floor.

"I think you've had a little too much whiskey." Orien laughed and clapped the man on the shoulder as he blinked around in confusion before nodding. "Stay here. Don't move until the dizziness passes."

He turned and walked back up the stairs, wiping at his mouth with one finger. Valentina understood his needs, but he didn't like advertising them to her.

The tavern was quickly growing busier, and he had to dodge several people before he found his way back to the table where Valentina sat waiting. He slid into his seat and reached for another whiskey at the same time she did, shivering as the heat from her skin sank into his.

Without pausing, Valentina slid the alcohol into her mouth, swallowing and then wetting her lips in anticipation. She knew as well as he did that the chase was fun, but the catch was better. He drank his whiskey and stood, skin tingling in anticipation when she followed and a languid heat slid through his body, making his cock pulse and his gums ache despite his recent feed. One of the things he loved most about Valentina was her ability to hold her own. She was tall, though he still had several inches on her, and the smirk on her lips said this time was not going to be gentle. She reached for him and tugged him by the hand to the door that led to the stairs and rooms above the bar. The heavy wooden door fell shut behind them, and the sound of their breaths in the sudden quiet had his mind in the past, to the way she sounded when she was close to falling off the edge with his name on her lips—

They both moved at the same time, his hands buried in her hair, the darkly curling locks spilling through his fingers as he tugged on them roughly and heard her moan.

"Valentina—" he panted, and she silenced him with her mouth. Her lips on his feeding the electricity that coursed between them until they were pressed together tightly, desperate to relieve the mounting pressure. He slid his hand through the high slit in her skirt and squeezed her thigh as he continued higher, reaching around to pinch her ass and lifting her when she gasped against his tongue. Her breasts pressed firmly to his chest, and he could feel her nipples tightening, hear the sweet thud of her pulse increasing as she moved harder against him, nails pinching into the skin of his neck as she nipped at his lip.

Light spilled over them as the door behind them opened and a muttered apology slid around them as the patron walked up to the rooms. Orien paid them no mind, simply gathering Valentina in his arms and carrying her up the stairs as she continued to grind against him.

"Need to get these skirts off you," Orien growled as he fisted a bunch of the offending material in one hand and Valentina bit his ear, trailing kissed down his neck before leaning back against the door to the room she regularly rented.

"Do you?" She smirked.

For a moment he could only stare at her. He slid one of the hands gripping her around the waist back down to the parting of her skirt, over her thigh, higher, groaning when he found her bare of any other obstacles. She gasped as his fingers trailed over the sensitive flesh just a few inches below where she really craved him to be, lingering and teasing while she cursed him through ragged breaths. He ignored her with a dark smile, content to let her writhe and beg. Her hand found him through his leathers and squeezed in a way that had him coming out of his skin.

"Wicked, wicked, woman," he purred, punctuating each word with a harsh kiss to her neck, teasing himself, and he could tell from her fluttering pulse that she liked the hint of danger that came from taunting him. He let a hint of teeth scrape against her as he skimmed the tip of his finger over her and groaned to find her soaked for him.

"Orien—"

"Inside, now."

She fumbled blindly for the doorknob as he kept his

hand on her, working her clit until her cheeks glowed red and her eyes grew hazy with lust. As soon as they were inside, he pushed her onto the bed before the door even clicked shut behind them, ripping her skirts off at the seam of her bustier and grinning with a savage delight at the sound it made as it bared her long legs. He sank to his knees and immediately hooked one over his shoulder. Valentina propped herself on her elbows and looked at him, breathless with anticipation. He didn't dare look between her legs, not yet, knowing he would cave to desire the moment he did. Instead, he tauntingly stroked through her folds, pressing a little firmer on the centre of her with each pass and relishing in her gasps of pleasure until she pushed her hips restlessly against him.

"Ren," she begged, girlish voice gone husky from want and giving an unintelligible moan as he sank his finger deeply within her.

"Like that?" he asked innocently and curled the digit as she cried out her assent. He added another and slowly began moving, barely holding back his own moan at the feel of her silky wetness against his hand. He couldn't resist. He glanced down and watched, hypnotised as his fingers pumped into her, and he groaned her name as he sank in again. He pulled the fingers free and brought them to his mouth as their eyes met, her lips parting as she opened her thighs wider in invitation.

"I need to see all of you."

Valentina didn't move, so he reached down and

tore through the front of her bustier with his hands and strength alone, feasting his eyes on her as the material fell to either side of her creamy skin and bared her breasts and stomach.

"I liked that dress," she said with a pout that had him imagining her lips wrapped around his cock. His trousers tightened almost unbearably until he was forced to take a step back and unzip them, stepping out of them quickly and shrugging out of his shirt too. "I'll get you another."

Her eyes travelled over the flush of his dark skin and the tight muscles spanning his chest before dipping down to the hard length of him. She stretched out a hand, her tongue flicking out to moisten her lips, and he bit down on his tongue as he stepped out of reach, instead sending shots of ice out to pin her hands to the bed.

Her dark eyes glittered in challenge, and his breath hissed out in anticipation as he sank to his knees once more. "I'll melt the ice if you promise to be good, Valentina."

Her eyes deepened at the sound of her name on his tongue, and she gave him a smile full of promise. "You know that's not within my capabilities."

Orien shrugged lightly. "Then I suppose I'll have to encourage you to be bad." He pressed his mouth to her clit and sucked hard, letting ice magick cool his tongue as he sent it over the moisture enticing him. Her hips jumped as he ran his tongue over the outside of her before plunging deeply within and she gave a hoarse shout.

"Ren, *Ren,* don't stop—"

He let his tongue flick back over her centre and traced his name with the tip of his tongue. She laughed as if she knew exactly what he was doing before the sound dissolved into another moan as he slid a finger in her, quickening his pace as he moved his tongue. Her hips moved uncontrollably, rising to meet his mouth and each thrust of his hand, and he felt himself become impossibly harder. He would have her, but first he wanted her to come with his name on her lips. He sucked lightly and sent ice over her breasts, teasing the nipples in a way he knew would border on painful, just how she liked it when they played this game. One more flick of his tongue and she pulsed underneath his mouth, letting out a breathy groan as she panted his name through the last quivers of her orgasm.

He didn't let her recover, releasing her arms from his magic and rising up to claim her mouth with his own. She tasted like whiskey and flowers, and he cursed as his cock slid up against her wetness, twitching in a way that had him closing his eyes for a second while he got his head back on straight.

"Are you ready now, love?" He panted as her hips began to slowly stroke him against her slickness. He lowered his mouth to her breast and nipped at the skin there gently before kissing away the sting, delighting in her pant of need. Her hand crept down to the apex of her thighs, and he caught it.

"Now, now, little bird. I didn't say you could come yet."

She whimpered and he growled at the sound. Orien pinned her hands above her head with one hand and smacked her clit with the other. She writhed against him, attempting to guide him into her as he resisted, content to torture her with lazy strokes as he kissed her, her body begging for release beneath him.

"Orien—"

He sank into her in one thrust before she could finish begging, flexing his hips as he sucked her lip. She opened herself up to him, moving her legs as wide as she could as he plunged in and in, until she called out, and he knew he wouldn't be able to hold off for much longer.

His hand skimmed down her waist, releasing her arms in favour of stroking one breast and pressing the other into her clit, letting his strokes match the deep pace of his cock. She tightened around him, and he gave a low groan, the hand teasing her nipple moving up to tug at her hair desperately as she came around him, moaning his name, and he fell apart with one final thrust, shuddering as he called hers in turn.

He slid out of her gently and laid down beside her on the plain bed, catching his breath. He felt boneless, utterly relaxed on a soul-deep level. Valentina could run from him all she liked but, eventually, she always ended up right here in his arms, giving into the call of her soul. The ceiling above them was painted a faded white and was cracked in places, but it was one of the more well-kept taverns he'd chased her to. The room was sparse, Valentina always travelled light, ready to run at a moment's notice, and the tattered remains of her dress tickled at his bare legs as he stroked her hair back from her face.

"Auren and Saiph will be here as soon as we send for them."

Valentina nodded, her face calm and peaceful, her body relaxed. "I'll be gone by dawn."

"Be careful."

"I always am."

CHAPTER TWELVE
AUREN

THEY ARRIVED IN SOMNIA AS THE SUN REACHED THE peak of its warm ascent. It had taken them longer than usual to traverse the Forest and she had teased Saiph mercilessly that it was because of her presence, that the Forest didn't like her. She hadn't seemed too put out by that fact, probably because at one point a particularly precocious tendril of darkness had jumped out at Saiph, knocking her down onto the hard forest floor and sending Auren into a fit of laughter as Saiph scowled.

The star was different than she had been expecting, ignorant in a lot of ways and gentler in others. Auren knew they were destined to be enemies. Saiph's mother did want her dead, after all, but she could not find it within herself to blame the daughter for the sins of her mother. In fact, the more she watched Saiph, the firmer Auren's belief became that there was hope for her yet.

She drew up her hood as they made their way out from beneath the trees that lined the border of Sommer and sighed at the sunlight that caressed her skin, as if trying to coax her inner flames to come play. It was hard, being inside the caves. She was grateful for the protection they provided to those who found their way to her, grateful even more so for the Forest which enshrouded them, but she missed the sun. Auren was able to leave freely, aside from Orien's nagging, but most of the others remained in the shadows where it was safe. Only the trusted could leave. Everyone else had to undergo a memory wipe, with the aid of the Forest's magick, to ensure their safety wasn't compromised.

Saiph glanced at her, dark eyes watching her seriously as she followed suit and drew up her hood. Even with her glamour intact, Saiph had trouble passing for human and, above all else, they needed to be discreet on this excursion.

Auren had the feeling the word wasn't in Saiph's vocabulary.

Somnia was very different to the north. Everything was brighter, the people happier. The south had been far less affected by the starfire attacks than the north. Auren could only assume it was Queen Fallon's ire that willed it so, given that the mountains in Viridis had once been her family's stronghold, the reigning seat of her parents.

As such, Sommer thrived while the rest of her people suffered, unable to cross the border thanks to the wide river broken only by the Forest that none dared enter for fear of the old magicks and creatures that dwelled within. They were right to be afraid. Auren had a certain amount of control over the darkness, but even she was not immune to its dangers. The river narrowed within the Forest, the waters looking strange, murky, and odd, but it was easily jumped to reach the southern half of her kingdom.

She began the descent from the trees, down a sloping hill where green grass tufted up between the light-baked earth. It was steep, but Saiph easily kept up, her long legs reaching further than Auren's, and soon the sounds of the market began to trickle in. It was perhaps what Somnia was most famous for—it was a cutthroat place that hid beneath a guise of glimmering fabrics and jewels, imported from oversea at the sole discretion of the regents, and meats so rich they'd made her and Orien vomit excessively the first time they'd tried them. After living off of what the Forest could provide for so long, their bellies had been unused to such luxury. The market was a fine place to find pleasure, or pain, equally.

The Forest's magick could shroud them for only so long once they'd left, but other times it would seem to beckon them, opening up exits through the trees as if to tell them it was safe—so they had drawn a most intriguing theory. Sometimes, the stars could not see them.

"You know," Auren said at last as the first of the

brightly coloured stalls appeared ahead, "this market is the place where Orien first met our source."

"Fascinating," Saiph drawled, and Auren fought back her smirk.

"Mm, quite. She punched him twice and robbed him blind before he could learn so much as her name."

Saiph's eyes sparkled as she looked at Auren, and she bit her lip on a grin of her own. She had rather thought that the star might enjoy that tidbit.

"Do tell. Your source is a woman?"

"Yes." Auren told her no more than that, and Saiph rolled her eyes before blinking in shock as the roar of the market hit them full-on.

It was a beautiful trap, full of colour and sound and scents that made your mouth water—or, at least, it did if you were half-mortal. But it was the night market that was truly where things had changed for the twins. It was more honest. More brutal. While Auren had been resigned to lurk in the shadows under Orien's orders, for her own safety, her brother had become something of an infamous face.

It started with a flesh trader, then a murderer, all in the name of the true heir, while the mortal regents Fallon left on the throne cast a blind eye. It was never meant to be a revolution, just justice. Vengeance. But Orien, however ill-advised, was making a name for himself. He was challenging the stars, the regents, and before long, they hunted for him. Auren knew he'd been back to the capital since, though many, many years had passed since that time, but this was her first time seeing the market since the day she'd forced Orien to return to the Forest, lest his recklessness be the death of him.

"Don't touch that," Auren said as Saiph reached out a hand to brush an amulet the peddler claimed could protect you from the sight of the stars. In reality, it was poisoned quartz. It seemed more had changed within the market than Auren might have guessed, the blend between the Night and Day merging to make a more dangerous place, wrapped in shadows of grey between the extravagant oranges and reds of the material that blew in the hot breeze.

"I'm immortal." Saiph reached for the stone again, and Auren hissed out an irritated breath, tugging the star onwards despite her cursing. "Wait. I said *wait*."

Auren ignored her, sliding easily through the gaps in the throngs of people.

"Stars-damned it, witch. *Stop.* Look."

Auren followed Saiph's nod of direction and saw three men. One was a pasty white, sweating excessively beneath the early sun, and she wrinkled her nose at the stale scent of him. The others were clearly Sommer natives, their skin a light golden tan that only made their companion stand out more. They stood huddled in the shade at the back of a vendor's stall, their eyes on a young woman who stood near one of the small fountains interspersed between vendors and the small bubbles she was making rise from the water with nothing but her mind.

"Fool," Saiph hissed, and Auren growled at her, making her jolt in surprise.

"Magick is not a shameful thing. She has every right to use it wherever she may please." Though, inwardly, Auren had to agree. Did this woman not know that their kind was being hunted? Snatched? Or did she think herself strong enough that it did not matter? An intriguing wager.

Saiph said nothing, her face darkening as the men continued to watch the woman.

The market stretched on for miles, eventually intertwining with the main cobbled street of the capital. Small stone buildings arched up on either side of the market as it wound on, and some mortals stood in the shade of them, smoking and chatting. Several alleys lead off to the side, and Auren knew that if they wanted to save the girl, they needed to act quickly.

Decision made, Auren spun away from the magick user and bumped deliberately into the man coming up behind them. His arms were full of woven baskets containing fabrics, his eyes barely peering over the top, and when they collided, he wobbled, falling straight into the vendor's stall to his right with a crash. Wares went flying, and multiple pickpockets moved in, temporarily obscuring the vision of the three men they'd spotted earlier. Auren apologised heartily to the man, managing to nudge a few other people over in the process and create even more chaos. Saiph, for all her faults, was quick on her feet, recognising the distraction for what it was. The air had stirred briefly at Auren's side as Saiph shot off, and she glanced up quickly to confirm the girl was gone before beating a hasty retreat into the crowd that was gathering to see what the fuss was all about.

In a market as busy as this, it was easy for her senses to become overwhelmed, so instead, Auren let the blood debt between her and Saiph guide her back to her star. She found them half a mile down the market, tucked into an alley. The woman was trembling, her eyes round with panic and then relief as she spotted Auren coming towards them. The alley was somewhat narrow and dark with a dead end that made her feel uneasy.

Saiph held the girl easily as she struggled, her hand clamped firmly over her mouth to drown out her screams, and Auren held up her hands as she approached, calling on her darkness to soothe their unwilling companion.

"Easy there, we're not going to hurt you." The girl's eyes filled with tears as she realised her saviour was working with her captor. "In the market, there were three men watching you."

The girl stilled, her tears faltering for a second as she jerked her head once to show she was listening.

"Others have been going missing. Others like us." Auren held up her hand and summoned her flames for good measure, and the woman relaxed further even as her bright blue eyes remained cautious. "We had to get you out of there before they took you. I'm going to count to three, and then Saiph is going to release you, okay?"

The star shot her a baleful look as the woman nodded. Auren counted down, and Saiph released the girl so suddenly she stumbled as she gasped frantically, bending double with her hands on her knees.

"What do you know of the disappearances?" Auren asked, and the girl stood straight, pushing herself back against the wall of the alley and looking between them.

"Not much. The same whispers float around. I thought it nonsense. Rumours." The girl's voice was husky, and Auren shot Saiph a reproving look—did she not say anything to calm the girl down once she'd snatched her?

"What are the whispers?" Saiph spoke in demands that, despite her better instincts, had several parts of Auren standing to attention, even as she wished sorely to truly fight that dominance with all of her own, considerable, power.

The girl looked warily at the star. "That more of us are going unseen, stolen away. They say it is in the name of the queen."

Anger licked at Auren's insides. How dare these low-lifes sully her name with such filthy depravity?

Saiph read her anger on her face and smirked. "You know nothing of real use then?"

The woman shot Saiph a look of incredulity as she swept her blonde hair back out of her face from where it had slipped out of her braid. "Maybe next time you should grab one of the kidnappers rather than the kidnappees!"

Saiph frowned and looked at Auren with a hint of suspicion pulling at her brows. "Excellent point. Auren, exactly what was your plan?"

She shrugged. "My plan was to save the innocent and then go back for the others."

"Really," Saiph said flatly. "Because it looks mighty coincidental to me that I could be well on my way to fulfilling our bargain at present, but instead I'm here. Stuck with you and none of the answers we sought."

Auren opened her mouth to respond but instead gasped as Saiph grabbed the woman once more, her dark eyes unfathomable beneath her hood and errant silver hair floating in the wind.

"Release me. Now. Our bargain was a life for a life. I saved her. Claim the debt fulfilled."

She couldn't do that. She needed to convince Saiph that the way forward was together. If she let her go now... Well, Auren didn't know what she would do. The woman whimpered in fear, and Auren's eyes met hers for a long moment before she looked back up at Saiph. "I do not believe you so cruel as to hurt her, *seren.*"

Saiph tightened her grip. "Release me."

"No. She is mine. She is under my protection. You cannot harm her."

Saiph laughed in a deep rasp, and Auren shivered at the glimpse of those fangs taunting her. "That clause is not without its limits, as you well know." Saiph tightened her hand until the woman choked, and then she smiled, secure in the knowledge that she could in fact, hurt the mortal. *"Release me."*

Auren couldn't. She needed the star. They didn't have much time to seduce her as it was and without Saiph, Auren would never be able to reunite the thrones. It was one woman versus the entire realm. Auren swallowed hard.

"You're not going to hurt her."

Saiph shook her head slowly, her eyes bleeding full black as her hood fell back and she tilted the woman's head to the side. Her long blonde hair tumbled fully free as she whimpered, water magick shooting from her hands and wrapping itself around Saiph's face. It would have choked her, had she needed to breathe. But the stars were not mortal. They did not sleep as the mortals did, nor eat. They were immortal, and this small display of magick would not be enough to rival Saiph's might.

Sure enough, the star waved her free hand, her flames instantly dissipating the water, and Auren took a step forward.

"Why won't you release me, witch? What is it you need?" Saiph's eyes were assessing as they ran over Auren's face. "If you tell me, I might spare her."

Auren remained silent even as the woman began to plead for her life.

"Last chance."

Auren tilted her chin upwards. "You wouldn't dare."

Saiph grinned and it was savage, bright teeth gleaming sharp and wicked. It should have been terrifying. "Watch me."

In a blur of speed, her fangs sank into the woman's throat and Auren clenched her jaw as the woman's whimpers gave way to a moan of pleasure. Saiph pulled deeper, the muscles in her throat working as she swallowed, and Auren's own, slightly shorter fangs, ached to snap out, to join Saiph on the other side of the woman's throat. The temptation was wrong. The woman's death was necessary, but she should not find pleasure in it.

The woman slumped, and Saiph dropped her to the ground as she wiped a smear of blood from her mouth and sucked it off the tip of one finger before stepping close to Auren.

"Next time," she whispered in a drawl that made Auren's hair stand up as the faint scent of blood and starlight carried to her, "I would just give me the information. Much less messy."

Saiph moved away, and Auren considered the body on the ground at her feet before setting her flames to it with half a thought. It was a dangerous game to be playing, and Auren wondered if she might have met her match. If she had any hope of her plan succeeding, she needed to up the stakes. Now.

"Come," Saiph demanded nonchalantly, not even glancing back as the smell of smoke filled the air, and Auren bit back her snarl at the order. "Let's hope our friends are still out lingering by the amulet vendor."

CHAPTER THIRTEEN
SAIPH

THE MORTAL MEN HAD VANISHED BY THE TIME THEY'D left the alley earlier that day, and Saiph had been... displeased, to say the least. Though, tasting the blood of the water magick user had helped soften the blow. All mortals contained a spark of magic that gave them life—the mortal magick users simply contained more of it, able to wield one or sometimes even two elements.

Saiph hadn't expected how much better their blood would taste though. It was like she was absorbing their magick as she fed. The blood of the mortal assassin now seemed like so much swill in comparison. In the Kingdom of Stars, the balls of ether were what provided their magic, burning for all eternity. When a star died, for they were long-lived, but eventually everything perished, their energy was released back into the ether that sustained them.

Now that she was on the mortal plane, Saiph

needed something else to supplement the natural ether she would normally get back in her realm. It explained the sudden bloodlust she'd experienced since arriving, and the more magick she used, the hungrier she became. It was an unnerving realisation, though. Saiph had never really understood her kind's need of fangs before this, but now it was clearer than ever—they were made for the mortal plane. At some point, probably lost to time, the stars and the mortals had likely existed here together, the magick in their blood a natural replacement for the ether-filled air in the Kingdom of Stars.

Re-energised from the feeding, Saiph could easily have kept searching the market all night. Auren's weaker, mortal body could not keep up with Saiph's own, however. So they had bought her some questionable smelling meat from the market and returned to the Forest, much to Saiph's dismay, and completed a thankfully much shorter journey to Eloria. Auren explained that Orien was waiting for them with an update, and they would rest at the tavern before journeying back to the caves.

They moved through the town towards the tavern. A sign above the door declared it to be *the best ale on this side of the northern border,* and Saiph's interest was momentarily piqued. She'd never tried human alcohol before and wasn't sure what sort of effect it might have on her. The stuff they had in the Kingdom of Stars was likely strong enough to kill a mortal.

The town they had passed through was in a much

better state than the pile of mud scrabbling to be a community Saiph had seen before her stay with the rebels. Camber, Auren had called it. A prickle of guilt tinged through her. So much progress destroyed at the hands of her people, her mother. Eloria had brick and wooden buildings in a slightly different style to those they'd seen down in Sommer. They were tucked together as if huddling for warmth all in a line, creating a dirt road through the middle that was broken up by a dry, stone fountain. Wheel tracks in the dust told her it was a popular enough town that they had a good chance of finding some information on their kidnappers.

Rows of houses sat one behind the other, some grander than others and glowing with lantern light placed in windows. The effect was cosy, despite the chill that blasted between buildings and the wind whistling. Saiph could taste a coming snowfall and almost smiled—it was yet another thing she'd never experienced. Everything in the Kingdom of Stars was so constant—darkness, starlight, moderately warm temperature—Saiph had never experienced warmth like that in Sommer, or blistering cold like this, nor snow. Even sunlight was a relatively new concept. Would her skin lose some of its ethereal glow after being on the mortal plane? No, Saiph likely wouldn't be here for long enough to find out. The timeline divergence between her world and the mortal would last a few weeks at most. Her time was running out. She was certain she would know the exact moment her mother could see them—especially if Saiph was still indebted to the queen's guard. She was certain her mother's wrath would shake the stars themselves.

A bell tolled somewhere close by, and Saiph jumped. She'd never heard a sound like it. The stars in the sky gave off their own frequency that was like music to her and, of course, the Kingdom of Stars were renowned for their musicality. Saiph herself had a passable voice. It was said that the stars were where the myth of sirens had begun, with legend telling that one note from the mouth of a star was enough to snare any mortal. She had never tested the theory and somehow knew this wasn't the time to try from the tight cast to Auren's eyes and mouth.

"What does it signify? The bell?"

Auren's hands squeezed into tight little balls before releasing. She kept her hood up and face tilted down despite there being no prying eyes that Saiph could see or sense.

"Remembrance. On this day one hundred years ago, Queen Fallon and the Kingdom of Stars slew the human Queen Tazlen, and her husband King Myrinn, alongside the infant heir to the throne, whose name has been lost to time… or despair, depending on who you ask." Auren's voice was flat and emotionless, but Saiph could sense she felt much, much more than that.

Confusion. Guilt. Love. The emotions made little sense to Saiph, but there was much more to the story here, especially considering Auren's version of events was deeply skewed, as they'd already discussed.

"An excellent day for the first star to be seen in centuries to be visiting then," Saiph said dryly, and Auren's mouth flickered into some semblance of a smile at that.

"Quite. Come, Orien must be wondering what's become of us."

Auren pushed past the tavern door, letting warmth and the smell of fresh bread drive out the sombre air between them as they stepped inside. It was mostly empty, just a few patrons at the bar and Orien lingering at a booth near the far end of the space, hidden in a mostly shadowy alcove. Auren's breath seemed to rush out all at once when she caught sight of her brother, and she signalled to the barkeep for a drink before rushing back to meet him.

Orien stood up with his own sigh of relief, wrapping Auren in a firm hug as he peered distrustfully at Saiph over her shoulder. His icy blue eyes seemed to have thawed a little though as he glanced back at his sister.

"Remembrance day," he said and pressed a swift kiss to her cheek. Auren nodded solemnly in return.

"*Victor Victis,*" she said, and Orien repeated the words before settling back down on one side of the booth. Saiph slid into the seat opposite and placed her back to the thick wooden wall, not wanting to leave herself exposed to the room as Auren now was. She seemed uncomfortable, but clearly had full faith that her brother would watch her back. The barkeep brought over two tankards of something that smelled like stagnant rainwater, and Auren withdrew the hood of her cloak once he'd left. Saiph followed suit, plucking up her tankard and sniffing at it suspiciously before taking a hesitant sip and cringing.

"*This* is the best ale on this side of the northern border?" Saiph gagged a little as the flavour caught on her tongue so she tasted it over and over.

Orien let out a chortle. "Fuck, is that how they're selling it now? Well, I suppose it would be the best ale since this is possibly the largest surviving town this side of the border. Easy to be the best when you have no competition." Saiph felt another stab of guilt, which made no real sense—it was not at her behest these attacks had taken place. "This is swill. The whiskey is much better."

"I do hope you didn't sample too much of it last night, brother," Auren said with no shortage of amusement, and Orien shrugged, the movement revealing a purplish bruise at the bottom of his neck.

"By the looks of things, you sampled much more than just the whiskey." Saiph smirked, and Orien tugged his collar up with a glare in her direction. "Did you obtain any useful information at all, or did I brave that unholy Forest merely to see the evidence of your sexual escapades?"

"Jealous, Saiph?"

"Not likely. Your sister has been keeping me *very* good company."

Orien's face turned a curious mix of both pale and red, and Saiph fought off a laugh, the realisation hitting her coldly in the chest. These people were her enemies. As soon as she was free of the blood debt, she *would* have to kill them. Laughing with them should never have been on the agenda, let alone fucking one. Orien apparently decided to let the comment slide, choosing instead to ignore Saiph completely as his eyes focused on Auren.

"Lips are sealed pretty tight, but whoever is doing this is doing it in the name of the queen." Orien's mouth tightened, and Auren looked equally perturbed.

"We heard the same," she said, and Saiph could tell it troubled her. "Did you find anything new?"

His shoulders lifted and fell in a half shrug. "We think someone must be tipping off the smugglers, at least on this side of the border. I spoke to some of the families of the girls taken—they were definitely all magick users, and the families were all dirt poor. They must *know* before they take them." Orien frowned as he considered what he'd just told them before he glanced up and scowled when he found Saiph's eyes on him. "Why is she here again?" he said, and a spark of anger curled in her gut.

"Well, the last time your beloved sister left the caves by herself, she came back crawling with assassins. I deemed it necessary for the blood debt to not allow that to happen again." Orien gaped like a gutted fish, and Saiph's lips curled in a smirk. "Oh, my apologies, was I not supposed to mention that?" she asked, directing the last at Auren, who met her eyes with a stubborn tilt to her chin that exactly matched her brother's.

"You did *what?*" Ice clouded the air in front of Orien's mouth, and Saiph watched with interest as his lips snapped shut and his eyes closed.

"No need to worry. I had my fangs in the little man's throat before he could say 'die.'" Saiph chortled, and Auren choked on her sip of ale as Orien's eyes flew back open as he watched Saiph suspiciously.

"You saved my sister's life?" Orien asked as he glanced between the two women. "Does that mean your debt is settled?"

Saiph considered it. "Likely not. There's no way to tell that Auren's life was actually in mortal danger from that piss-poor assassin. Besides, he said he was there to kill the heir, not Auren—we can test it out though, if you'd like?" she said with a taunting flash of her fangs and watched his face pale with some satisfaction.

"Put those *away*. If anyone here see's what you are—"

"Then I'll have myself a snack and be out the door before the humans can fetch their pitchforks."

Orien threw his hands up in the air, and Auren lightly cleared her throat.

"If you two are quite done? You know, I think your problem is that the two of you are too alike."

Both Saiph and Orien stared at Auren, aghast, as she delicately continued to sip at her ale.

"Us, alike? What—"

"Did the assassin get to you after all? Bash your head—"

"The darkness from that fucking Forest must have screwed with you—"

"*We are not alike.*" They finished in sync, and Saiph gagged in disgust as her voice rang out with Orien's. Yet, a surprisingly warm ball of *something* filled her chest. Was this what it was like? To have friends? Family that you could count on? Saiph had Vala, of course, but they were as different as night and day. She mentally shook away the unusually melancholy thoughts. One day, she would find her soul-bonded mate and have a family of her own. No pressures surrounding marriage or heirs would ever plague her as they weren't requisites of her kingdom. Given the star's long lifespans and difficulty conceiving children, the throne couldn't always pass to 'blood'—instead nominated heirs were named in the place of legacies. Unlike the humans whose very courts, when they had still had them, demanded heirs and spares and starlight knew what else. It was seen more as an honour than a requirement for a star to be picked by the Fates to conceive a child. Perhaps it was a lesson Saiph could pass on when she ruled this little slice of hell, she mused, lips twisting and enjoying the wary look on Orien's face as he tried to decipher what could have that particular smile on her mouth.

Finally, he swore, gesturing to the bored barkeep who brought over three small tins of an amber liquid that stung Saiph's nose.

"What *is* that?" Was it poison? Surely not, the blood debt between her and Auren would never allow it.

"Whiskey," Auren replied with a slight smile as she watched Saiph sniff at it.

"Or what passes for it in the North," Orien muttered. "It's much nicer down south in Sommer."

"We'll go back together one day," Auren said with a gentle smile, and the siblings exchanged a look Saiph didn't quite understand but decided to ignore in favour of the cup of fire she'd just inhaled. It burned through her veins with a sweetness that surprised her. It was nothing like the alcohol in the Kingdom of Stars. That was heady and thick, this was heat licking up her throat and making her pulse pound. She could feel Auren's eyes on her face and looked up to meet eyes that she now realised were only a few shades lighter than the amber whiskey she had consumed.

"You liked it," Auren stated, and Saiph smirked.

"I suppose I've found at least one thing on this plane that makes it redeemable—whiskey. Oh, and blood."

Orien spluttered, but Auren just laughed in a low, long way that had Saiph's stomach tightening in anticipation—of what, she wasn't sure, but she had liked the sensation a surprising amount. She had expected there to be tension between them after she had killed the mortal back in Somnia, but Auren hadn't said a word. Though there had been a certain shadow in her eye when she'd looked at Saiph that she couldn't quite figure out. Was it condemnation? Desire? The two looked surprisingly similar.

"Let's get back on topic." Orien huffed, and Saiph chuckled. He reminded her of a puffed-up birdlike creature she'd once seen in a tree while watching this plane, feathers ruffled as it hooted at the sky as if in hello. "We think that friends or family are selling the magick users to the smugglers."

"Why would they do that?" Saiph asked, even as a voice inside her head that sounded like her mother sneered *typical humans*. She had more loyalty in one fang than they did in the whole of their bones.

Orien growled, and Saiph stilled, something in her recognising a predator and giving her pause as she reassessed him but found nothing amiss. "You have *your* kingdom to thank for that! They're poor and starving. Eloria is the closest town that holds a market to buy the food they now can't even scavenge for unless they want to brave whatever creatures roam the Forest—but they have no gold."

"So they give the smugglers their family members, friends, lovers, for *gold*?" Saiph snorted derisively, and Orien's jaw grew tight with anger. He exhaled sharply out of his nose, but Auren interrupted before he could say another word.

"They are fighting every day, *seren*. It is not just gold, it is *survival*, food for their children, the promise of another sunrise with a full belly."

Ice slid through her veins, and she opened her

mouth to say something, anything, but Orien beat her to it.

"I can't imagine you've ever known hunger like they have, not living up there in your fancy kingdom tucked in your nice, warm bed."

"You," Saiph said, danger coating her tongue as her fangs threatened to descend, "don't know *shit* about my life."

Orien leapt across the table, knocking Auren's ale flying in a shower of yellow and foam as Orien's fist slammed into Saiph's jaw. She welcomed the pain, eager to finally have this out with the arrogant mortal.

"They cannot *live* because of *you*, because of *your mother*. You selfish, arrogant—"

Saiph's hands closed around his throat and cut him off with a gurgle as he choked, the skin of his throat casting a shadow onto her skin as Orien stamped on her leg with his foot, and she let go of him with a yell as the bond attempted to wrangle her. He slammed back into her, grabbing her stupidly long hair and slamming her face into the table, once, twice, before she whirled and snapped his head up with the force of her punch, and trickles of lightning flowed through her as the bond rioted. Orien howled as his blood sprayed, and Saiph paused as an odd scent rose up—

"*Enough.* You've caused a scene and made me spill my ale." Auren hauled Orien up by his ear and he winced, scrubbing the blood from his nose off of his face with some water magic. "Go fetch me another." She turned to Saiph with a raised eyebrow and offered her a hand that Saiph accepted as graciously as she could muster as pain spun through her body in tiny pinpricks that felt like needles.

"You mustn't bait each other, *seren*. You don't want to hurt my brother, not truly, else I imagine the bond would have truly felled you."

Saiph rolled her eyes, opting to ignore the witch and the pain that still had her firmly in its fist.

"I know," Auren said before Saiph could speak, "that to be true *because* of that fight just now. I saw you in those smuggler's tunnels. You were as fast as lightning, deadlier perhaps. You held back with Ren, and I'm grateful."

"I didn't want to blow our cover," Saiph muttered, but Auren just smiled and hummed an acknowledgement.

"He's wrong, you know. I know what it's like to starve, to live in filth. My mother's training was… very well-rounded."

Auren clearly didn't know what to say to this, her mouth opening and closing again as Orien returned with her ale, setting it down with a thunk and a glare.

"So," Auren said, apparently deciding she would need to take control if they wanted to stay on track. "What are our next steps? We saw some smugglers back in Somnia, but they got away before we could question them."

"Our… source," Orien said after a brief hesitant glance at Saiph, "is going to run a ruse for us, act as if she needs the coin and is willing to trade for it if need be. She'll feed the information back to us, and we'll be waiting for them when they come."

It wasn't a half-bad plan. The only thing that rankled Saiph was that it was the only plan they had.

"How will they contact you?"

Orien pulled Auren's drink towards him and took a sip. "This will be our rendezvous point. As soon as they give me the info, I'll send word, so be ready to leave and meet us here at a moment's notice." Auren nodded tightly, and Saiph could see she didn't want to leave her brother here in this place without her. His eyes softened as they scanned Auren's face. "I'll be careful." His eyes slid to Saiph and he gave her a slight, and surprising, nod. "Look after her."

"I will."

"Good," he said, slamming Auren's now-empty tankard of ale down onto the wooden table. "Now get some rest and leave before first light."

Auren stood and pulled the hood of her cloak up and then moved to cup Orien's cheek, turning away with only a nod and marching towards the door that had to lead to the rooms above the bar. Saiph tugged up her own hood and paused, intrigued, as Orien opened his mouth.

"If anything happens to my sister, I'll kill you."

Saiph grinned at him, baring her fangs and meeting the challenge in his gaze head on.

"If anything happens to her, it's because I'm already dead."

Orien nodded but said nothing more, sipping his

drink as he cast his eyes about the bar. Sensing his dismissal, Saiph turned and stalked across the wooden floor and up to the door that was swinging closed after Auren.

She wasn't keen on staying here in the unsecured tavern where anyone could be waiting at any moment —though, of course, they would find themselves in a sticky situation if they busted in and found themselves on the wrong end of a star.

At the very least, she was grateful for a night not spent underground.

Saiph followed Auren into a room at the top of the stairs and immediately headed to the window to peer out at the night sky. Regardless of the veil between their worlds, the stars were still visible, and Saiph let out a slow breath as she traced their familiar constellations with her eyes.

She turned around and froze. The room was fine, if plain, but what gave her pause was the sight of Auren, the buckles on the leather armour that tucked up under her breasts undone and the laces of her blouse loose and trailing at the front, offering a tantalising glimpse of bronzed skin. This in itself made Saiph's mouth run dry. But then her eyes moved to the moderately sized bed that stood in the centre of the room, mostly sheer four poster curtains hanging down on either side and tied off to a bedpost.

Part of her was excited to get in a real bed, rather than the mattress she'd spent little time on in the caves, unable to sleep. The rest of her was horrified, though perhaps not as much as she should have been, to realise there was *only one*.

"What are you doing?" Saiph's voice came out in a croak, and Auren threw a look up at her as she moved to the buckles across her hips and slid them free, shimmying the hard exteriors down over her thighs and then peeling off the warm under-leggings to reveal only the smooth expanse of skin, save for the scar on her thigh.

"Getting ready for bed. I recommend you do the same. It's been a long day."

Auren brushed her long hair back over her shoulder as she finished undoing the buckles on her waist. The white fabric of her shirt hung around her as the guard slipped off to join the rest of her armour on the floor. The slit at the front of her shirt gaped wide, and Saiph swallowed hard. What was wrong with her? This was her enemy. *Her enemy.*

Auren, another voice seemed to whisper. *Just Auren.*

Saiph thought that might be worse. The witch was a fortress of secrets, each likely deadlier than the last. It should have been off-putting, maddening, instead it was... intriguing. She knew Auren was playing her, knew she had some agenda, but maybe it was time Saiph got some answers of her own.

Auren lifted her arms as she raised her shirt from the bottom, exposing her taut stomach and full breasts, nipples tightening in the cool air, and Saiph found that she couldn't breathe. The witch's hair thunked down onto her back as she finished tugging off the top and dropped it to the floor before glancing nonchalantly to Saiph, and she wanted to laugh.

This was to be a seduction, then. What secrets of hers did Auren long to expose? What weaknesses? It was a game Saiph was more than capable of playing, so she let her voice turn husky as her hands dropped to her own trousers.

"You should cut your hair."

Auren blinked, startled. "What?"

"Your hair," Saiph said as she placed her swords under the bed and shrugged out of her top. There would be no fanfare to this removal of clothing. It wasn't how she operated. Besides, she wanted to catch Auren unawares. All the better to capture her secrets.

She rounded the bed in a blur of speed, and Auren shivered lightly in the breeze Saiph left. She sank her fingers into the long, gently waving tresses and then yanked hard until Auren's throat was exposed. Saiph stepped close, letting her breasts brush against Auren's as she leaned down and whispered into the witch's ear, "You should cut it off. It's a liability."

Auren breathed heavily, and Saiph wondered how long the witch would let herself be held in such a vulnerable position, considered if maybe she might enjoy the dominance of it.

"Noted," Auren said, and Saiph hid her smile as she released the witch in a long glide of her fingers but didn't step away. Instead, she moved closer, until their bodies were flush and the warmth from the heir's guard seeped into her as she roughly grasped her chin and tugged it up to meet her gaze.

"Tell me to stop," Saiph teased, and Auren said nothing. Maybe she was shocked that her little game had turned on her so thoroughly, or maybe she still thought she was in charge. Saiph laughed darkly and didn't hesitate, capturing the witch's mouth with her own in a savage, biting kiss that made her growl.

Auren's hands slid over Saiph's bare hips, stroking upwards and closing over the peaks of her breasts before moving faster than Saiph could have expected and closing her hand around her throat.

Saiph chuckled, and Auren's smile was all dominance as she threw her down on the bed, straddling her as the hand on her throat moved back to her breast, and hot kisses trailed over the place on her neck where Auren had gripped her.

"Tell me, *ignis*, what is it you wish to know?" Saiph murmured, and Auren's kisses faltered for a moment until her mouth dropped down and closed around one nipple, laving and sucking until Saiph's back bowed up from the bed. "Are you planning on fucking it out of me, whatever it is? I have to say, I've experienced worse forms of torture."

Auren remained silent, though her thighs flexed, pinning Saiph's hips in place as she moved over to her other breast, nipping at it lightly until Saiph swore. But when Auren finally spoke, it was not the question Saiph expected.

"Tell me, *seren*," Auren murmured as she sat up and

hovered her body over Saiph's, "have you had many lovers?"

For a moment, Saiph just stared and then she laughed, not having expected Auren to be quite so good at the game as she. That was easily resolved, though.

"Perhaps I should be asking that of you," Saiph said, sliding her fingers over Auren's shoulders and cupping the back of her neck. "After all, you seem terribly familiar with your tongue." Saiph flipped them and Auren gasped out a laugh as her leg hooked around Saiph's in an attempt to take back control. Instead, she grabbed it, hooking Auren's leg up and around her hips and nudging her other thigh open fully as Saiph drank her fill.

"You know, you really are exquisite," Saiph breathed, tracing her hand up and over the scar that ran acrossAuren's leg and waist, sensing as much as seeing that it was magical in nature. It shone silver in the low-light and, before Auren could respond, Saiph dropped her hand to the apex of the witch's thighs. "If you answer my questions, you'll get a reward." She circled one finger around Auren's clit for emphasis and smirked at the wetness she found waiting for her.

"And if I refuse?"

"Well, that's just no fun for anyone, now is it?" Saiph pressed down firmly onto the small nub begging for her attention, and Auren's hips bucked slightly before she got them back under control. "How about this? Answer a question, and you can pick your pleasure."

Intrigue lit Auren's amber eyes, and Saiph wanted to crow with victory. So the little mortal enjoyed both domination and dominating. It would be a useful tool in her arsenal.

Saiph teased her for a moment more, using her own thighs to pin Auren's in a reversal of their earlier position, making her smirk as she slid a finger down and dipped into her briefly, taunting shallowly. "What is it you want from me, witch?"

Auren gasped, trying to writhe as Saiph's hand continued teasing, and eventually lifting her own to stroke along her sensitive edges before Saiph sent out a tendril of magic and pinned Auren's hands to the bed.

"No answer? A shame," Saiph said as she leaned down and pressed a long lick to the sweet and musky wetness in front of her. "I had been so looking forward to doing this. But only good little witches get to feel my tongue." Saiph pulled back and slid a finger deeply into Auren's wet heat, curling the digit and rubbing at the sensitive wall there until the witch cried out.

"Are you searching for my mother's weaknesses?"

Auren panted lightly, but her eyes were clear and bright when they met Saiph's. "No."

"Well, there's really no way to measure the validity of that," Saiph said thoughtfully. "I'll give you half a treat just in case." She added a second finger and pumped them in and out quickly as Auren attempted to press down on her hand. Saiph tutted lazily, feeling her own wetness gathering between her thighs at the sight of the witch spread out before her like the most sinful offering she'd ever encountered. This was wrong, no question about it, but she wanted it anyway. Wanted *her*.

"Are you going to try to kill me?" she asked next, and Auren stilled, an unexpected fire blazing in her eyes at the question. "Interesting," Saiph murmured, knowing the answer even before Auren told her. Whatever secrets the witch held, she did not wish her harm. At least, not directly. "Ask your pleasure then, *ignis*."

Auren's voice was hoarse as she tried to speak with Saiph's fingers still sliding inside her. "I want to see a real queen take the throne."

Saiph paused her hand's motion, unsure what this meant, until Auren smirked.

"So please, *Highness*, come and take a seat."

A tendril of delight swept through her, and Saiph's fangs longed to sink into the tender flesh in front of her, but she held back, knowing that wasn't the game at hand. She withdrew her fingers but left the bands of magic in place as she moved lithely to part her thighs for Auren's mouth.

"This is what you want?" Saiph asked breathily as she straddled the witch's shoulders, placing her hands against the warm skin of her chest.

"More than anything," Auren whispered and Saiph wanted to groan, knew she likely would in a moment's time as she faced the head of the bed and sank down onto Auren's mouth.

Her tongue ghosted across her wetness, and Saiph hissed out a breath as her hips jolted once, twice, and then steadily rocked against the tongue that rubbed against her clit. Auren moaned beneath her, the vibrations making Saiph's hips sink lower, needing *more*, until suddenly a tongue was pressed to her entrance and driving in with enough force and delight to make her breathless.

She looked down and met Auren's golden gaze as she ground down against her mouth, rocking her hips as they held eye contact until Saiph moaned loudly and pulled herself away.

Auren gave a cry of protest until Saiph span around and released her hands in one fluid motion before seating herself with enough room to devour Auren in turn.

Her first moan made Saiph impossibly wetter, the slick sounds of their pleasure rising in the room as their hips rocked in a perfect rhythm of desperation, each racing to drive the other off the edge first.

Saiph longed to sink her fangs but resisted, instead sliding a finger deep inside Auren as her tongue and mouth sucked at her clit relentlessly. Auren cried out, defiantly feasting on

Saiph in return until Saiph was forced to relinquish her hold on the pleasure building inside her.

She slumped between Auren's thighs, panting as

the feeling of relaxation immediately took her, and she eventually heaved herself up and rolled away.

They lay side by side, breathing heavily in the near dark until Saiph spoke.

"I don't trust you, little witch. But I don't hate you either," she said softly, not caring in that moment if to say so was treason. To consort with a mortal... her mother would strip her of everything of value if she knew.

She could hear the smile in Auren's voice when she replied. "Sleep, *seren*. There will be plenty of time for you to hate me later."

CHAPTER FOURTEEN
SAIPH

THEY HAD MADE THEIR WAY BACK TO THE CAVES through the darkness of the Forest in silence the next morning. Saiph would have given her left fang to know what Auren was thinking at that moment in time. They'd awoken tangled together, naked bodies still warm from rest, and hadn't spoken beyond Auren's cursory observation that they needed to leave. Had their tryst last night been a mistake? Perhaps. But she felt better for it all the same, as though it were a line in the dirt that they had crossed, trampled, and spat on— but they had done so together.

The feeling was surprisingly nice for all that it changed nothing. Saiph still had her orders, and Auren still owed allegiance to her own queen.

Saiph worried her lip between her teeth, suddenly unsure of herself and irritated by the feeling. She'd had plenty of lovers in her almost hundred years, but none had left her anxiously contemplating their meaning after their time between the sheets.

The bond felt different today, too. Like it had solidified its chains even more securely around Saiph's wrists, binding her to the woman she should hate, the witch she would have to kill.

In the quiet of her own mind, Saiph could admit she disliked that fact—but a fact it remained. She huffed a sigh of frustration, feeling her thoughts running in a circle, and Auren shot her a bemused look as they trudged onward.

All they had to do now was bide their time until Orien's source was able to ferret out the information they needed to lay their trap and truly begin their hunt. Anticipation tingled through Saiph in a rush that had her breath hissing in a little differently. For most, the waiting they were now subject to would most likely be dull. For Saiph, the build-up was all part of the chase. Perhaps it was easier for her because she did not experience time the same way the mortals did. What was a week or a month of waiting compared to eternity? Though, Saiph could admit she was eager to have the smuggler's blood on her tongue and would prefer that to happen sooner rather than later. She gave a small shudder of longing and felt Auren's gaze linger on the side of her face again for a breath.

Suddenly, the darkness surrounding them parted like a cloak and Saiph blinked in surprise as air free from the oppressive magic of the Forest found her lungs. The time had passed much faster that time, she was sure.

"Why didn't it make things that fast the first time?" Saiph huffed as they stepped out from beneath the foliage, and Auren smirked.

"Because you irritated the magick living there the first time."

They climbed up a steep formation of rocks to reach a ragged ledge, and Saiph gazed out over the mountains and cursed Forest. From up here, it was almost peaceful. Just her and the wind and the scent of earth strong in her nose. Auren wrapped a hand around Saiph's and tugged impatiently and, with a sigh, Saiph prepared to go back beneath the earth once more, casting a quick look around to ensure Auren wasn't returning dripping in assassins again. Everything was still, the Forest unnaturally so, and she scowled at it before following Auren through the rocky entrance that had appeared with a well-placed push of her hands. *Now we wait.*

SAIPH HAD SPENT the last two nights stalking around the tunnels, attempting to map them out in her mind— but it was almost impossible! They branched and twisted off one another, making it difficult to tell where one ended and another began. If she hadn't known better, Saiph would have thought they were moving.

She'd seen no sign of the heir, and that had put her in an even fouler mood when she'd found herself back in a loop at the bathing caves again—despite the fact that she'd headed in the opposite direction already. Twice. Steam curled around the edges of the flap acting as a door to the baths, and Saiph looked at it longingly. Kara had found her when she'd returned and only really left her side when his mother bade him. Except for today, when he had declared that she smelled so strongly, his delicate nose could know no more torture.

Saiph grinned to herself in the lantern light. The small human was oddly endearing. Of course, she'd never admit that to Auren, who would tease her mercilessly—but it was all but hardwired into Saiph's being to like children, or at least to admire them for the miracle of life that they were. Her mind turned, unbidden, to the nonsense claims Auren had touted as fact—that Saiph's mother had slain not only King Myrrin who was kin, but also his heir. It was part of what made it so unbelievable. Queen Fallon couldn't be described as maternal, but even she had attempted her duty to the survival of their kind and ended up birthing both her and Vala.

She shook off the thoughts and surprising melancholy and headed into the bathing chamber. Saiph was mostly certain that Kara had been teasing, but it wouldn't do for the heir to the throne to be as filthy and unkempt as the mortals she would one day rule.

This was where Auren found her almost ten

minutes later, an expression on her face that Saiph had never seen before and was having trouble deciphering. It was… sly, but hesitant.

"I thought I'd join you," Auren said, her husky voice loud in the mostly empty chamber. It was the first real words she'd said to Saiph since the night at the tavern. "You don't mind…?" She was moving before Saiph could answer, shucking off her leather pants and tugging her cotton top up and over her head in one smooth motion.

Saiph gestured to the bubbling water with a little bemusement. What did she want? A repeat? Saiph wasn't sure that would be wise. She'd never felt the passage of time before, but she was more aware of it than ever recently, knowing that her time with Auren was growing short and her chance to fulfil the blood debt perilous.

"Did you need something?" Saiph asked as Auren dipped a foot in the water and let out a breathy sigh of appreciation at the heat before sliding the rest of her curvy, bronze body in.

"Maybe," Auren replied, as if that were an actual answer and not just more vague bullshit. She waded her way closer until Saiph could see the steam beginning to dew on her eyelashes and the droplets of perspiration that trickled down her throat, her chest. Saiph cleared her throat lightly and looked away, startling slightly as warm fingers brushed against her hand, and Auren smiled slightly when Saiph turned back to her.

She smiled at Auren with her fangs freed, and a strange light seemed to flare brighter in Auren's eyes, the intensity of their gold deepening. She ducked under the water and slicked her hair back from her face as the silence grew between them.

Auren tugged at a sodden lock of Saiph's hair, examining it between her fingers, its brilliant pale standing out in sharp contrast to her warm skin. It was sheer vanity that had made Saiph keep it as long as it was—hazardous, perhaps perilous as she'd warned Auren, and as Orien had proved the other day in the tavern. But with each stroke the Queen's guard pressed into her hair, Saiph found she couldn't bring herself to regret keeping it long. Auren drifted closer, and the water swirled lazily around them, like they were caught in the eye of their own personal storm. She slipped in behind her, and Saiph fought to remain still, the predator in her not so sure that giving Auren access to her unguarded back was a good idea, but then she relaxed as Auren's fingers trailed up her spine in a lazy caress that made her shiver.

"Cold?" Auren breathed, her voice sending goosebumps over Saiph's skin as much as the air. She felt Auren's power stir, and the water grew even hotter, steam beginning to curl thickly through the chamber, obscuring them from view.

"Tell me about her," Saiph murmured softly, ignoring the provocative note in Auren's voice as her own echoed strangely through the fog, needing a distraction and a reminder now more than ever. "Your queen."

Auren's fingers stilled momentarily before rising and resuming their gentle untangling of her hair. Vala would call this folly, Saiph thought idly as Auren's hands stroked from root to tip, to let a mortal's hands so close to her throat... but Saiph was no fool, and Auren likely would not need her hands if she wished to end her. That was the thrill, to be so tantalisingly close to potential danger, to have it quicken your breath and tighten your breasts, to feel possibility nipping at your heels, flirting with your pulse as it pounded nearer—

"Once upon a time," Auren's voice shook through her thoughts like a dash of cold water, and Saiph let herself relax against her, the picture of trust as she rested her head against Auren's bare shoulder and peered up at her, throat bared. Auren's eyes burned down at her, no doubt noting the submissive gesture and choosing to ignore the temptation Saiph was presenting.

Even for a mortal, the need to dominate, to rise, had to be strong, and for Auren to wave it off... Saiph wanted to smile. This creature was born for power. She likely would have done well among the stars if not for the misfortune of her mortality.

Skin slid hotly against Saiph's back, and she wondered briefly just how far she would be able to test Auren before the truth of her dominant nature overtook her. Saiph let a spark of fire slide from her palm and skitter over Auren's skin, heard a sharp intake of breath and felt the hand against her hair clench slightly and then relax.

"Once upon a time, there was a lost queen. She had no throne, for it had been stolen. No family, for they had been killed, and no equal, for she was wholly unique." The water sloshed lazily at Saiph's stomach as she stretched, letting her eyes slide to half-mast like a cat, missing only a purr of satisfaction. As if this wasn't prized information, even if it was biased. To find the heir, perhaps Saiph first needed to know a little more about her—to better understand the threat she presented to her mother's throne. When the water stilled, Auren continued.

"War had ravaged her lands for many years, or so it had been told to her, for she was but a blink of starlight when the violence reached fever pitch. The stars were envious of their mortal cousins, for though the stars' steady brightness held a beautiful glow, they did not burn as vividly or love as fiercely as those with finite mortality."

Saiph scoffed lightly. She had asked for the tale of the false queen, but she had not expected a fairy tale. Auren ignored her except for a sharp, reproachful tug on the lock of Saiph's hair in her hands. She could hear the smile in Auren's voice when she continued. "And so the two kingdoms warred, until a star fell from the sky. It was Prince Myrinn—prince no longer."

Saiph startled at the name, Auren's hand clasping softly on her shoulder to ease her back into stillness.

Myrinn. So this fairy tale did have some truth to it then.

"Myrinn had become King of the Stars and, unlike his father, he sought peace—not war with the mortals. He had a proposition for the human Queen Tazlen, for it was always the females of the line that ruled, much to her brothers' fury. He offered this: The unity of the kingdoms. An end to the war. His hand in marriage. But the two soon fell deeply in love."

Saiph's heart thudded too hard in her chest. This was her history. The story of how her mother came to be queen. How she came to be the so-called villain. And Auren was *butchering* it. Did the mortals really trust in such theatrics? A star and a mortal wed with love?

Auren's hand rubbed wet, lazy circles into the skin of Saiph's shoulder as though she could tell Saiph's patience was beginning to wear thin. Her skin had begun to cast a soft glow and there was a sudden tension present, like a rubber band stretching impossibly tight between them.

"Queen Tazlen agreed to Myrinn's proposal," Auren's voice was low enough now that even Saiph's hearing was strained. "It had been agreed by the *Balteum* that King Myrinn would marry the mortal— and their kingdoms—together."

A knot began to grow in Saiph's stomach. This was more detail than she had ever before heard about their complicated history with the humans. All she knew was the council of stars had tried to create peace, they sent their most beloved King Myrinn, to the mortal plane, and all they got for their trust was death and savagery at the hands of the mortals. It was why mortal and star couplings had long been outlawed, though until meeting Auren, Saiph had been unable to understand why anyone might *want* to lie with a mortal. It was a harsh seduction, one that had felt inevitable and yet infinite.

Saiph's mother would understand the need to do anything to get what they wanted, and if she didn't, if Saiph happened to enjoy herself at the same time…

"But not everyone on the *Balteum* was happy about this union, believing humans to be little more than animals, inferior, unworthy. So, as King Myrinn married Queen Tazlen, a plan was hatched—a coup."

This was outright fallacy. This was not the way the histories went. And yet…

They are unworthy of our light, my heir. Savages that live by the grace of our hand.

"There was a year of peace and prosperity, the Kingdoms of Sky and Earth brought together as one. A princess was born, heir to the Heavens and the Earth both."

"What was her name?" Saiph rasped, unsure why she cared, except she had a terrible feeling that more than the timelines diverged between the two kingdoms. Had the truth been warped too? But for whom?

"Nobody knows," Auren murmured, waving an absent hand through the coils of steam that surrounded them. "It has been lost to time."

"Impossible," Saiph declared, catching the hand

Auren still swept in the air and running her fingertips to her elbow in a trail of tickling heat. "Your queen cannot be so old as this. I am surely triple your years, and this is before my time."

Auren ignored her words. "It was when the princess was nearing her first birthday that they struck."

"Auren—"

"They had whispered and conspired, deciding which laws could and could not be forfeited in their quest for power, for greatness. Until at last, the light of half the *Balteum* was extinguished and later that day, King Myrinn and Queen Tazlen too."

Saiph shook her head and pushed herself away from Auren, chest heaving as she pulled in stiflingly hot breaths, the water sloshing angrily between them. "You are mistaken. Tales of fanciful fallacy cannot belie the truth in our laws—*we do not kill our own.*"

Auren's hand curled into a fist, and her eyes burned hotter than Saiph had ever seen them, a flame engulfed in darkness, flickering and raging against the night. Her brown curls clung to her forehead and flushed cheeks, dried in the steam. Her lips begged to be bitten and power surged between them, Saiph's fangs aching to drink her, to claim her.

Seeing the usually cool and collected Auren succumb to rage was like nothing Saiph had seen before. Nothing like she'd hoped. The sensation ran through her, like cool air brushing against sensitised skin, like starlight dripping from her body, hypnotic in its danger, fantastic in its depth.

"The mortals betrayed us," Saiph said, both to correct her and to stoke that fire a little deeper, longing to see it explode, longing to see Auren's own teeth go for the jugular. A dangerously thrilling provocation. "They killed their monarchs in the dead of night and blamed us, but we knew the truth."

Laughter bounced eerily off of the cave walls, the glow worms shivering as it brushed past them, creating a ripple of light as Auren pushed around to face Saiph once more. Her eyes burned like molten bronze, and Saiph knew she was close to letting it all go. To shedding her skin and showing Saiph what she was really made of. "The newly orphaned queen and heir was smuggled out of the castle and taken deep into the Forest, a place of old magick where even the stars could not watch."

"Auren, it is not possible. The babe was slayed. Even if she were not, your queen would be dead of old age, or at least too withered to raise a rebellion."

"Then why did your mother send you?"

Saiph raised and dropped a delicate shoulder. "To quell unease, to reaffirm her power. *Not* because she thinks some pretender has a right to a throne that doesn't exist here anymore, nor the one in my own kingdom."

Auren's lips quirked, and Saiph knew she'd lost her, that the explosion she'd sorely hoped for, the reveal of the secret she sensed buried deep, was firmly under control once more. She continued as if Saiph hadn't spoken. "The queen waited in the Forest as the years passed, training and learning, sneaking to speak to the villagers in small snatches as she learned what had become of her kingdom. Until at last, she was ready and could emerge to claim her thrones. *Victor Victis.* To conquer the conqueror, the spearhead of the coup—Queen Fallon."

Saiph didn't look away from her smouldering gaze. "You speak only in falsehoods and riddles. You are a fool." This was a waste of time. Her *mission* had been a waste of time, hunting for a queen who didn't exist, and now, with her time on the mortal plane drawing to a close, this fallacy would spell her death.

"My queen," Auren said quietly as she rose from the water, body glistening as rivulets slid down gold skin, "rules all."

Had Auren ever even seen her queen? Had Saiph failed in her search of her because she did not exist? Disappointment slid through her, that she could have been so taken in by this mortal who was just as much a fool as the others. *Queen's guard...* maybe self-declared, for Saiph had finally reached the conclusion that the queen existed in spirit only. A clever ruse, because how could you kill an idea?

"Your queen is dust on the wind. You rally behind a memory."

A smile ghosted across Auren's mouth as she climbed from the pool and looked down at her. "You had better hope so, *seren*. Because my queen is half-star, and you do not hurt your own."

Auren's words hit like punches to the stomach. Half-star. Not mortal. The blood, if it even existed, had bred true? *You do not hurt your own.* Her mother couldn't have believed this fallacy to be true, could she? She would not have sent Saiph to kill another star, even one with a claim to the throne. But... Saiph wondered. Her mother was bloodthirsty, with little warmth or virtue or honour but a kin-killer? Saiph's heart felt like it beat sluggishly.

Would Saiph recognise a fellow star? What Auren now accused her mother of... not only the cold-blooded murder of half the *Balteum* and the King, but in conspiring to do so again...

Saiph should kill her now. To protect her mother, for the slight—she didn't know. But she knew what her mother would do in her place right now.

Saiph didn't move, and the water stilled as Auren walked away.

Kin-Killer. It was a serious accusation and, if Auren was right, was Saiph risking the label by killing the false heir? Was it even appropriate to label her as such if Auren's tale was to be believed? Or maybe it was all just more human lies and manipulation. Had her mother hoped Saiph wouldn't recognise the false queen's heritage when she encountered her, or had she believed it all to be fallacy? What would Saiph do if the queen truly was the bridge to peace between the kingdoms? Kill her? As her mother, the queen, bade?

Perhaps that would be for the best regardless. What truths could this woman unveil about the stars?

One week. That was all she had left of the timeline divergence to break this deal and discover the queen's whereabouts, if she even existed. But if she did—*when* she did, could Saiph really kill her?

The spark of humanity combined with the immortality of the stars, something wholly unique. Humans who once had full starlight in their blood were all but gone, and even then, none possessed the ability to create starfire. That was a power passed almost exclusively through the royal line.

That would have to be it—a trial by fire. A worthy heir would not burn and would wield the flame. A pretender would become ash. Still, the question remained, bitter in her thoughts and on her tongue.

When her mother had sent her to kill the false queen, had she known she was sending Saiph to kill a star?

CHAPTER FIFTEEN
VALENTINA

THE MARKET SQUARE IN SOMNIA WAS CROWDED THAT morning despite the chill that had begun to creep into the southern border. They'd likely had their last glimpse of the warm weather several days back, the river that separated the north and south now too cold to dip in your toes. Soon it would freeze, and those bold enough to risk the ice would likely meet their end from the patrols that doubled, the regents unwilling to let in too many travellers lest there be more hungry bellies to fill. Of course, there were still ways to enter Sommer… if you knew where to look or the right people.

Men hollered about bread and cheese while others peddled useless pieces of stone or rock said to keep the gaze of the stars turned away from your fate. Valentina snorted. If there were such a thing in existence, starlight knew she would have long since claimed it.

Perhaps it would buy her a credible head start against Orien. A soft warmth built in her chest at the thought of him and she sighed, rubbing at the skin of her chest that she had on display. Star-damned soul bond.

Valentina loved him. Logically, she knew that, even without a soul-bond confusing matters. Her hatred of the stars far outweighed her fear, but she could only pray for Orien's sake that it continued to be weathered against the force of her love for him. The bond was inconvenient though, making her stressed, sloppy, if she went too long without contact despite them never taking that last step to solidify what lay between them. Her soul craved him, and there was very little to be done about that, though perhaps it would not keep driving her into his arms quite so much if she just accepted her fate and let him sink his fangs.

Ducking between stalls of cured meats, she swiped an apple off of the table in front of her, hiding it deeply within her skirts as she held them aloft in one hand as though afraid of the dirt on the ground. When the peddler's gaze moved on from her breasts, she tossed the apple to a scrawny child lingering in the alley opposite and staring hungrily at the tables. They caught it and bolted, and a small smile twisted Valentina's mouth—when she was that age, she would have likely done the same. The streets were not kind to children on their own, even those in 'built-up' towns like Eloria in the north. If anything, it just made the penalty for theft stronger. She'd met Orien in an alleyway just like the one before her now, while she'd still been working as a pickpocket. Many men looked at her and saw only her beauty. Ren was perhaps one of the few who also saw her cunning—though it had done him little good. She'd still thrashed him soundly and stolen all his coin.

She'd watched several people in the town speaking to one man in particular at a small stand on the outskirts of the market. This in itself wasn't unusual, but their behaviour was—the small glances shot over shoulders, the tension lining their hands and jaws... what were they so scared of? The man's stall was a plain wooden table with tent-like curtains draped over more wood to shield him from the sudden cold. A small fire burned in the corner, and she couldn't help but eye it longingly. Her fingers felt frost-bitten, and she was almost certain to lose a tit if she had to parade around in this get-up for much longer. It was an unfortunate, but necessary, evil and the easiest way to keep a man distracted while you extracted information or fleeced them of their gold.

Many of the people who visited his stall full of worthless trinkets left empty handed, but several times Valentina had spotted the tell-tale glint of gold pressed between passed hands. If someone knew anything about the disappearances of the magick users, it would likely be him. He looked brutish, with a thick nose and thicker hands, but Valentina smiled prettily as she swayed up to the table.

"Oh, such a *big* fire you have there—I'm a little jealous. I fear I may catch a cold at any moment." Valentina wanted to vomit at the high, simpering voice that left her mouth, but the man likely wouldn't have even noticed—not with his eyes glued to her chest. She pressed a hand to it for full effect as she said as breathily as she could manage, "Though even when I'm home, it's not much better. What good is having a fire-wielding magick user for a cousin if they can't keep you warm in the winter or earn you any gold, hm?"

The man was blinking slowly but gave a grunt at her words. "Travesty."

Irritation flared through her, and she fought to keep her voice controlled. It was hard. She was growing tired of this life, this role. "I truly *wish* there was a way I could utilise them to their full potential."

The man was staring at her, a hint of suspicion hiding in the narrowing of his eyes, and Valentina dropped the act with a sigh of relief, realising it would get her nowhere with this man. He may have been interested in what she had to... offer, but her feminine wiles were getting her nowhere. "Look, I need the gold, and I heard that you were someone I could come to an arrangement with."

"Half up-front and half on delivery," he grunted with a voice like gravel that made her feel vaguely nauseous as he attempted to clear it once, twice, before finally spitting on the ground. She tried not to cringe and wasn't sure she succeeded as she nodded briskly. He pressed four gold coins into her outstretched hand,

and she almost swore. Even without delivering on her end of the deal this would be a tidy day's work—was this a scheme she could try multiple times if there were different liaisons to talk to? She pulled her thoughts back and away from her greed, but the man seemed to have spotted it on her face and smiled grimly in satisfaction. His teeth were yellow and blocky, and Valentina steeled herself against the lascivious lick of his lips with his thick, white tongue.

"Where—"

"Not here. Viridis. The square by the bell tower. Ten chimes, two days. Make sure they're alone."

Valentina nodded, slipped the gold into her brassiere, and tugged up the hood of her worn cloak before making her way back to Eloria, to the tavern where Orien would be waiting. On horseback, it would likely take her several hours but it was faster than walking without the aid of the Forest. She dared not enter it without Auren or Orien at her side.

The guards at the city gate were familiar faces, and they nodded at her when she came into view, looking hopeful beneath the hoods of their cloaks. She flicked the closest one a gold coin, and he gave a low whistle as he held it up to the sunlight that was rapidly fading.

"A good day for you then, Birdie?"

Valentina wasn't entirely sure why she'd told the guard that name the first time she'd approached these gates astride her mare. She'd had Orien on her mind and the name had flown out, she supposed. She had a myriad of aliases she liked to use, but Birdie was the only one that simultaneously filled her with both irritation and longing. Still, it paid to be on good terms with the guards in the regent's employ, especially when she needed someone to watch her horse. Animals did not last long in this world of hunger.

She waved goodbye to the guards as they hauled open the gates and lowered the bridge for her to lead her mare across and, once she'd reached the earth on the other side, she swung her leg over and began to ride.

Long ago it might have been considered inappropriate for a woman to ride astride her mare, but with so much darkness and change in their world, some traditions fell away. Much for the better, she believed. Though the kingdom had long since been ruled by women, prior to their current overlords, that is, Valentina could not fathom living in a world that refused her trousers for fear of the shape of her legs.

The towns she passed through were little more than rubble. Camber seemed to have grown worse every time she laid eyes on it. Oddly, it reminded her of home, of Astor, where she'd lived before her parents had died in an attack of starfire. Everything reduced to so much ash around them.

Eloria was doing well compared to some of the other towns, though its fountain ran dry and the market grew sparse. Valentina kept her head down and ears to the wind, trying to stay ahead of information and make use of any that could benefit Orien and Auren. Things were getting worse on the outskirts.

Hunger had always been rife, as had disease, and Valentina had experienced both at a young age before making her own way in the world. They couldn't carry on like this.

Buildings laid crumbled, ash still thick in the air, and what remained of the villagers hovered around small campfires and makeshift tents, their eyes dead and cheeks hollow with hunger, and she did not slow as she rode through. Valentina had been half tempted to chance the Forest rather than go through the town in her old cloak that likely seemed the height of riches to the remainder of their village, a temptation many could not refuse. She knew it was a similar story in many of the smaller towns on the outskirts of the kingdom. Once she reached Viridis proper, she stashed her mare in the old barn she'd come to view as her own. It was out of the way enough that not many would know it was there and close enough to the edge of the Forest that most people would not have gone near anyway. Ren had helped her when she'd shown it to him, urging the forest to grow over the roof, enshrouding it in darkness. Valentina brushed her hand down the mare's nose and walked over a bucket of rainwater before she left.

Somnium had once been a thriving kingdom. The last noted period of peace and prosperity was under Myrinn and Tazlen's rule—Orien and Auren's parents. Since then, Somnium had been absorbed into the Kingdom of Stars, the land of dreamers almost wholly forgotten in the rise of blood and fire that had since consumed everything. Queen Fallon was nothing if not thorough.

Some of the towns in the Southern continent had fared a little better than those of them in the North. Food wasn't as scarce, people still had homes, and creativity wasn't a waste of time. The colours, the warmth... The north had a quiet and natural beauty that was rapidly being destroyed by the Kingdom of Stars with each attack of starfire. Sommer had remained largely unscathed compared to the mass terror in towns and villages in Viridis like Camber, who'd had most of their inhabitants wiped out by the wrath of the stars.

Yet, Sommer had not completely escaped tragedy. The reigning regents active in Sommer had been killed on the same night as Myrrin and Tazlen and replaced by those Fallon had deemed more malleable to keep up small amounts of overseas trade and control. Far less was known about them and even fewer things remembered. All of her attempts to glean any information hit dead ends, but she felt instinctively that they would not find any allies there, not after the way they had pursued Orien several years ago. The death of the regents sometimes struck Valentina as almost worse than the notoriety of the king and queen's deaths—for at least they were remembered, their names murmured on each Remembrance Day. Those regents had been lost to time and theory, and sometimes Valentina wondered if she might end up the same way if Orien and Auren didn't succeed in reclaiming the throne. Lost to the passage of time like so much dust on the wind.

She shook herself from the melancholy thought and tugged her cloak around her a little firmer as her breath made fog in the air. The monarch's seat of power had always been in Viridis, the remnants of their fortress stronghold now bare in the mountains and half-collapsed. Perhaps it was why the people remembered so much more in the north. History had happened *here*. Though the accounts were still not enough to properly encapsulate the horror that had occurred and was likely warped between truth and myth and bias. It was fortunate, in a way, that the twins remembered very little of their time with their parents, being no more than babes. She had to imagine it hurt less that way. Valentina could remember her own mother quite clearly and often wished her memory might fail her just a little more so that she might not have to remember the frailness of her hand or the delicate blood on her lips when she coughed. In the end, the disease hadn't even the chance to take her.

Some said Queen Fallon attacked the north with so much more vehemence than the south because of what it represented—human power and the power of the sky and earth united. Valentina snorted as she made her way down a dark, winding alley that would take her to the tavern. The Kingdom of Stars and their sadistic queen didn't need a reason to want to destroy the mortals. Just their continued existence was enough —yet, she had never made to wipe them all out completely, Valentina mused. Though, she supposed there was still time yet. Queen Fallon sending the heir to Somnium didn't bode well. The threat Auren posed had finally caught her attention, and Valentina could only mutter a prayer that they all made it out alive.

Footsteps scraped softly behind her, sending dirt and pebbles skittering, and tension bled through her veins as her heart beat faster. To run would be foolish, especially if the smugglers had her followed. Maybe she had seemed too desperate, too eager in the marketplace, but she had to imagine they all were if they'd resorted to selling out their family, their friends. Valentina carried on, letting her feet hit the ground evenly, the *clomp, clomp* of her leather knee-highs reassuring her. She was not a victim. She could hold her own in a fight. Something she'd learned the hard way and refined with Orien and Auren.

Valentina rounded the corner of a nearby building and breathed a small sigh of relief as the tavern came into view. The glow of lantern light guided her way, and she only dared a small glance back as she reached the door. The darkness of the close-packed dirt streets was still, and her heart finally seemed to slow. She reached for the door handle with a little more confidence and didn't make a sound as she watched out of the corner of her eye as a shadow peeled away from the wall of one of the houses across from her and walked away.

Orien was seated in the booth in the corner of the large room and made to stand as he saw her sweep through the entryway. She gave him a minute shake of her head and glanced meaningfully towards the windows that lined the front of the inn. Instead of joining him, she strode purposefully towards the bar and smiled at the barkeep. Hennick knew her as a regular and often passed on interesting pieces of information that he picked up while working. It was amazing what people let slip after some cheap booze and easy company. His face was wisened, deep wrinkles ploughing through the skin of his cheeks and mouth, but his blue eyes were alert as he assessed her lightly shaking hands and bloodless lips. She hadn't even realised she had been pressing them together so tightly, but her mouth ached as she exhaled a ragged breath. No wonder Ren had seemed so concerned when she'd come in.

"Easy night out there?" Hennick asked quietly as he passed over a tin tumbler of whiskey. It was the same thing he always asked her, but there was an undercurrent of urgency in his words that was new. She let her eyes raise to meet his own and unclenched her jaw.

"Little windy tonight, actually."

"Trouble?" he asked, and she shook her head.

"Shouldn't be. They stopped following me once I got to the door."

A frown deepened the creases of his face, and Valentina let herself relax incrementally. She'd known Hennick for years now and, in a lot of ways, he was like the father she'd never had. He looked out for her, and even if there was trouble, Hennick would never turn her away.

He gave her a slow nod. "Well, you know where I'll be."

Valentina couldn't stop the soft smile that spilled over her lips. "Oh, before I forget," she slipped a hand beneath her cloak and dug around in her brassiere for one of the gold coins the smuggler had given over. "Here, my tab and board for this week and last."

Hennick looked amused as she dropped the slightly warm coin into his hand. "Do I need to check where you got this?"

"I didn't steal it, but even if I had, you'd know better than to turn it down." She laughed, and he agreed with a fast smile and nod of agreement. He poured her another whiskey, and she nursed it at the bar while her toes unthawed and her emotions settled.

"What about your... friend?" Hennick asked as she stood to make her way to her room.

She gave him a grin. "Let him pay for his own board and drinks, starlight knows he's always trying to buy mine."

Maybe it wasn't wise to bait Orien, for he had undoubtedly heard every word of their conversation with his heightened hearing, but perhaps it would teach him not to eavesdrop else he might hear things he didn't like. Valentina smirked to herself as she made her way to the stairs that led to her room. She didn't need to look to know Orien would follow—though he'd likely wait a small while to ensure whoever had followed her wouldn't become suspicious.

Her room was cold when she entered, the dark space holding a few too many shadows for her to be comfortable, and she hurried over to the fireplace and stoked a fire in the grate. The room quickly grew warm, and she sighed in relief as she tugged the thin curtains across the window after peeking outside and finding everything still. There was a small bathing chamber within her room, and she shucked off her cloak, tossing it carelessly onto the wooden chair that sat next to the fire before making her way inside to splash her face before bed.

The water had barely dried when her door opened and closed so quickly she'd have thought she'd imagined it if not for the fact that Orien now stood in her room.

Orien's icy blue eyes were bright as they ran over her form quickly. He closed the gap between them in a blur that made her gasp. She wasn't sure she would ever get over how quickly he moved. His hands on her bare arms were warm as they ran down to clasp her hands.

"Are you okay?"

For a moment her tongue was tied, and she could only nod, caught in his stare. She had been gone just over a day, and yet the bond between them was pulled taut, as though it despised every inch of space between them. Orien shuddered lightly as his hands moved to cup her face. Valentina had gone into the town each afternoon, a few times dipping into the more well-to-do shops like the seamstress' or the small bakery opposite, but she'd had no luck until she'd ventured out at dawn to Sommer. She wasn't sure if the fire that now burned inside her meant their bond was getting stronger considering it had been such a small time apart— maybe all the time they'd been spending together had done more harm than good. Except, bond or no, Valentina couldn't deny that it was nice to end the day in Orien's arms, to have somewhere to curl up that felt entirely hers—safe, warm, and loved.

"What happened?"

She took a small step back until his hands dropped away from her face and gave him a smug smile. "I found the contact. He had a stall in the market, and Ren... I can see why people are going for it. He gave me four gold coins. *Four.* People could feed their family for at least a year with that. And he said I'd get the other half on delivery. I used two coins to pay off the guard at the gate and Hennick, but we need to be careful. If they've got these sorts of resources, then we could be biting off more than we can chew." The only people she could think of that might have had *that* much wealth were the regents, but what did they stand to gain by removing the magick users from Somnium?

Orien nodded as she spoke, worry lines creasing the space between his eyebrows, and she turned away so she wouldn't smooth them. Testing herself, needing to know how much of what she felt was the bond and what was her—though she supposed it made little difference, they were essentially one and the same. Orien was always meant to fit the gaps of her soul. The Fates were cruel mistresses, indeed.

"Did they give you a time and a place?" he said at last, and she nodded with her back to him as she pulled open the ties on the front of her top and unhooked her belt, setting them all on the side next to her cloak before turning around. Orien swallowed, tongue wetting his lips as he moved a step forward as though hypnotised.

"Clock tower, ten chimes in two days' time. He said to make sure they come alone."

Orien nodded like he heard her, but his gaze was on her mouth, and the hands fisted at his side were tight with tension. She understood, because her body ached for his, her soul aflame in his presence as their bond drew them together. Or was that just lust? Love?

"Valentina—"

"I'm tired, Ren. Maybe you should go to your own room tonight, in case someone is still watching." She regretted the words as soon as they sprung out, but she wouldn't take them back. She needed space, needed to know her choices were her own and not just Fate driving her towards some end goal she wasn't sure she agreed with.

Orien nodded slowly. There was fresh hurt in his eyes that she felt just as deeply, as though wounding him was the same as hurting herself. He stepped forward half-hesitantly before taking her in his arms and squeezing once. His lips ghosted across her forehead and left the skin there tingling.

"Be safe," he said and was gone, the breeze from his passage and the soft click of the door as it shut the only proof he'd been there at all.

CHAPTER SIXTEEN
ORIEN

ORIEN AWOKE WITH HIS SHEETS TANGLED AROUND HIS hips and his bed unusually cold. He'd become accustomed to waking with Valentina curled around him, her dark hair soft against his arms and tickling his nose, her floral scent lingering on his skin. He worried about her, more than just their bond gnawing at him as soon as she left his side. What they continually asked of her put her in danger, and while he knew logically that she could take care of herself, he still didn't want her to get hurt. Valentina was right, whoever was funding this was powerful if they were offering that much gold up front just for the *chance* of capturing a magick user.

He sighed and rolled out of bed, cringing at the cold wooden floor against his bare feet and hoped he would be able to avoid a splinter from its rough surface this morning. Orien made his way to the window and tugged the curtain back, blinking blearily at the sun that was just about peeking over the tops of the rows of houses in front of the tavern. To his relief, he couldn't see anybody lurking outside, and he drew the curtains again as he went to freshen up before finding the only messenger he trusted to get a message to Auren.

The day was ungodly cold, even for him, and Orien found himself missing the warmth of the caves —though it was hell in the summer months. Condensation would drip from the walls, and the air would be so thick that at least one of the children would collapse before mid-day. But when winter hit, the caves were cosily lit with lantern light, and the small nests of fires tucked into nooks and crannies kept everyone pleasantly warm.

He also missed Auren. It was lonely sitting in the tavern all day listening to the locals, and it wasn't often that he spent more than a week away from his twin. The whiskey helped, but in honesty, he was bored, and it was hard watching Valentina going out and risking herself while he sat by on the sidelines, waiting. He'd reached the point where he'd be glad of any company, even Saiph's—which was lucky, considering she would be accompanying Auren when they received his message. It had been... fun, before, in the tavern. There weren't many people who could keep up with him in a brawl, and it had been refreshing to not have to hold back as much as usual—though keeping his fangs in check had been difficult, especially with Saiph's proudly on display and taunting his every instinct. Auren could keep up with him just fine. She was more magically gifted than him for a certainty, but his strength was greater than hers. He'd caught a glimpse of her expression while he and Saiph tussled on the floor, and it had been bemused, resigned, something soft there for a second before she'd walled it away. More than being left here to wait, he worried what might be happening back home.

That Auren had come home trailing an assassin and *Saiph* of all people had been the one to dispatch them rankled. It was his job to protect his sister, the future queen—as it was always the women who ruled, which suited Orien just fine. He wasn't made for the clever schemes and political balancing that Auren mastered so easily—relished, even. There was a part of him that wanted to ask her how things were going with the heir. Was she close to winning her heart? Did she truly think this was a viable way to claim back the kingdom from the rule of the stars now that she had actually attempted it? He knew it was too risky to mention these things anywhere in Saiph's vicinity, but what truly held him back was that he wasn't sure Auren would tell him the truth. His feet hit the dirt path towards the town square a little harder than necessary, and he struggled to rein in his ire.

She often withheld information to protect him, giving him what he needed to know only when she deemed it necessary, and it was hard to have a twin who kept so much hidden. Was she lonely? Scared? Orien wasn't sure he knew any more. He blew out a breath as he rounded the corner, and the bell tower came into view just as it chimed nine times. There was definitely something between her and Saiph though, had seen it in the way Auren's body twisted towards hers just so, and the sly look on Saiph's face as she taunted his sister mercilessly. It could just be lust, or even just a mutual respect for the power Orien could feel sequestered within them both. Perhaps Saiph appealed to Auren in the same way she did to Orien— the relief of someone you didn't need to be careful around, someone you didn't need to pull your punches with or be careful not to break when you fuck. The scar that wound over his chest, neck, and shoulders began to tingle, and he rubbed at it absently. That day had been when things had changed between him and Auren, when she'd started protecting him instead of fighting with him.

"AGATHA WOULD HAVE HAD our heads if she'd caught us doing this," Orien mused as he whipped off his shirt and threw it onto the forest floor.

"Well, unfortunately she's no longer here to protest," Auren said with an unusual amount of venom, and he raised his brows at her. It had been just over a year since Agatha had become ash on the wind, a result of their own carelessness and Agatha's reluctance to tell them the whole truth about what hunted them. They had since learned much, digging deep into their own histories, visiting the tomb that had once been their home, and slowly piecing together the information their nursemaid had seen fit to impart.

"Yes, how inconvenient for us that she saved our lives from a

lethal bout of starfire that wouldn't have been present if we hadn't left the Forest's shroud."

As if the Forest knew they were talking about it, the tendrils of darkness surrounding them deepened. The old magick here was strange, even seeming sentient at times. There was a lot to learn about this world they'd never been able to be a part of, and the Forest seemed inclined to help. Just like him and Auren, it too was utterly unique and almost alone in the world. Perhaps that gave them a kinship, or maybe it was just that there were perks to being the only full-blooded half-stars, half-mortals to exist of the royal line, that they knew of, anyway—like immunity from the madness the Forest's magick often seemed to conjure in mortals. They'd unfortunately learned that lesson the hard way. Sometimes, a gap would open in the darkness, letting in sunlight, and he and Auren would know that it was safe to leave and gather information on their parents, the kingdom and, above all, their enemies. Auren theorised that there were times the stars could not see, just like when they remained in the Forest, and that the magick knew this and sent them out while it was safe. They charted the gaps and found a pattern—Auren had been right. Any other time they left the Forest and used their gifts, starfire would shoot through the sky and they would hurry back to the shroud of darkness that protected them. Here they could practise their magic freely, both mortal and not, for they could not see the stars any more than they could see them.

Auren's jaw was clenched, and magic sparked at her fingertips. She had become more and more untethered the past few weeks, her magick more unpredictable, the fire in her eyes blazing all-consumingly. He sighed and moved several steps back. She would tell him what was bothering her in time, but he hoped it would be sooner rather than later. It wasn't healthy for her to bottle up all her emotions.

"Come," he said, and Auren attacked. Ice rushed past his fingertips in a glimmering wave, meeting Auren's flame and twisting in mid-air as they grappled and twisted. He shot blades of ice either side of the whirling mass and watched them turn to harmless steam as they met Auren's shield of heat. She was strong and only growing stronger, as if she was able to draw down into a bottomless well of power that Orien himself couldn't follow. He scraped into his own significant reserves and channelled more energy into the dragon of flame Auren had set to roaring. Something changed. His ice burned fiercer and colder, alight with a burning blue light that he could only stare at in awe.

"Starfire," Auren breathed. Her golden eyes seemed light again for the first time in a long time, and they let their magic fade out at the same time. "Agatha wasn't lying. Only those descended from royalty are able to wield the starfire, Ren."

"I didn't realise you'd thought she had lied."

Auren shrugged. "I don't know who to trust, other than you, of course."

"You saw what happened to Amelie when we tried to bring her to the Forest, Auren, and the way Aggie herself seemed to be unravelling. We wouldn't still be standing here if we were regular mortals. Aggie didn't lie."

"I know, I just had to be sure." Mentioning Amelie had been a mistake, Orien realised. The hardness was back in her gaze, her nostrils flaring with anger. This was what had been bothering her.

"Auren—"

She shook him off. "Enough, Ren. Let's go again. We need to be stronger."

"Stronger for what?"

Auren looked at him incredulously. "Have you not been paying attention? Our kingdom is being held hostage by the woman who took everything from us—our parents, our home, Agatha... it's our responsibility to take it back."

"You want revenge."

"Don't you?"

"You can't survive on anger and vengeance alone, Auren."

She looked away from him, into the endless dark depths of the trees before turning back. "I want to help our kingdom too. The throne is ours—"

"Yours." Auren blinked in surprise, her mouth opening in protest, but he shook his head. "The women are first in line to rule, it's custom, and if we want to free our kingdom, then we need to do it right."

"You will stand with me then?"

Orien smiled and waved her forwards. "I would follow you into the Heavens themselves."

A grin curled Auren's mouth, and he blinked at the small fangs that gleamed white against the dark. It had been a shock when they'd first appeared, and the sight of them still took him aback. They were learning more about themselves every day, and with nobody to teach them what to expect, they didn't truly know what they were capable of. They'd always been able to see in the dark. Agatha had found it endlessly irritating while she stumbled along, tripping over tree roots and they strolled as though it were daytime—not that there was ever much of that in the Forest. The fangs though, those were relatively new, and he was feeling a little worried as to what he might need them for.

Magic slipped out of Auren's hands, curling around them in a circle of flame that rose so high he could feel its heat on his neck. The trees always remained unscathed after they sparred, and Orien had to wonder if it was the old magicks that resided here that protected them.

He knew what was coming next—shielding. Auren was much better at it than him, and her magic lasted longer. The flames encircling them would stop any magical blow-out, sending any trees soaring if the old magick should fail. Magic burst out of Auren in a wave of red and gold, curling and spitting as it prepared to test him. He focused on his ice, on the coldness of winter, the bitterness of loneliness and the ache in his heart for everyone they'd lost already. His shield was strong. Thrums of starfire ran through it in thick veins that had him gaping in awe, and Auren's eyes sparkled with excitement.

"I'm going to give you more than usual. I want to see how much the starfire changes your shield." Orien nodded, and Auren's flames grew thicker, hotter. His shield did not give.

"It's holding—" He glanced up at Auren in excitement, and alarm shrieked through his body at the glaze in her eyes, her pupils blown out, entirely caught in the thrall of wielding the magic. "Auren!"

Her head flew back in ecstasy, and she raised her arms higher, the flames following her movement and rising high above their heads in a blazing dome that rapidly began to change, flaring white, blue, gold, and then silver. It was like pure lightning edged in flame, like Auren's very essence was pouring out of her with no end in sight.

"*Auren, you need to let it go! It's going to burn you out!*" He was shouting now, the roar of the flames so loud he was sure he would hear it in his dreams if they both survived this night. Auren shuddered, and her eyes that had flickered closed, opened. Arms trembling, she attempted to lower them, but the power flared brightly in her eyes and she groaned. He ran forward and paused only at her warning shout.

"*Stay* back! *I'm trying to rein it in.*" Her words were slurred, and panic ate at his insides. He couldn't lose Auren too. She screamed, and he couldn't hold himself back any longer, rushing forwards as the tower of fire surrounding them tried to pour back inside her, forcing her head back and her arms out as it sank in and then exploded outwards.

He didn't remember hitting the ground. Cool darkness enveloped him, and his eyes fluttered as he watched tendrils of darkness reach out and smother the last of the flames, able to interfere now that Auren's shield was broken.

Frantic hands pressed his cheeks, his forehead, and he could feel something wet trickling down his face. He grimaced as his hearing seemed to return to him all at once, hadn't even realised the blast had deafened him until Auren's voice came to him.

"*Ren, Ren, I'm sorry, so sorry. I didn't mean to, wake up, wake up——*"

He opened his eyes and frowned at Auren. She was on her knees with her face pressed to his chest as she sobbed. He lifted an arm with considerable effort and dropped it into her hair, attempting to soothe her as pain radiated through his chest. She sat bolt upright, pressing her hands back to his cheeks as she scanned his face.

"*Thank the stars, I thought I'd lost you.*" She sobbed harder, *and he pulled her to him, settling her against his side and pressing her hand to his chest so she could feel his heart beat.*

"Lose me?" he rasped. "You truly think I'm that easy to kill?"

She didn't laugh, and Orien shivered. She felt too hot pressed to his side, like the fire that had escaped her had burned her up inside.

"Stars, Ren, you're freezing."

She pressed a hot hand harder against his chest, and he gasped in pain as electricity and ice flashed through his senses. Auren sat up, wincing as she clutched her leg for a moment before tugging aside the burned material of his shirt and gasping. He looked down and felt his mouth drop open at the large scar that radiated down over his shoulder and chest. It was bright white against the midnight of his skin and felt icy cold to his touch.

Auren's eyes were wide and full of tears once more. "Your magic healed you. I could have—you were almost—"

"I'm fine, Auren."

"But I almost—"

"I'm fine. I'm not so sure we can say the same about you, though. Your magic... it's much stronger than mine. If the starfire inside my veins is a drop, then yours is like the ocean. You need to be careful. My magic may have healed me, but if yours is the reason you're self-destructing, you might not be so lucky."

Auren stood and stumbled slightly, making him frown as he reached for her. "I need to go."

His eyes widened. "Auren, I can't go anywhere right now and your leg—"

"No," she said simply. "Just me. I'll be back, but I can't— I can't be here right now. I won't leave the Forest. I just need

some time, okay?" She didn't wait for his answer before backing away.

"Auren, wait!"

Her footsteps faded away quickly as he lay unmoving on the floor, pain lancing through him in pulses. Soon all he could hear was his own breathing and he closed his eyes, left with only the darkness for company.

CHAPTER SEVENTEEN
SAIPH

THE TAVERN WAS MUCH BUSIER THE NEXT TIME AUREN and Saiph stepped foot inside. The journey through the Forest had passed in a blur, but Saiph had still longed to swing Auren up onto her back and run through it as fast as possible—which was considerably faster than a mortal could move. Things were... not tense, exactly, between her and Auren, but it seemed as if Auren was waiting. For what, Saiph wasn't sure. An admission of guilt? A sudden repentance and decision to change allegiances? The air between them felt a little heavier than usual. Though, Saiph could admit that maybe that had more to do with the tightness of her throat and her inability to stop her eyes from straying over the pulse in Auren's throat every few moments.

Auren cleared her throat, and Saiph tugged her eyes up and darted them around the inn. Men and women alike crowded the bar, but Auren took her arm and pulled her past, leading them to the same booth in the back that they had met Orien at before. Interesting that they met here often enough that he had a regular table. The booth came into view and Auren beamed up at Orien in a way that made Saiph's blood rush through her body a little faster. There was a flush of warmth on Auren's cheeks that had Saiph biting her lip. All these foreign sensations and desires were becoming a true nuisance for her goals. Someday soon Saiph would likely have to kill Auren to get to her queen, and she didn't want things to become complicated by anything as trivial as sexual attraction. It would only end badly.

Saiph pulled back the hood of her cloak, nobody likely to notice her in this crowd, and made to sit down before stopping short at the woman that sat before them. A true beauty, with a spill of raven curls and deeply dark eyes. Her mouth was full, red and pouty, and she had a surprising amount of creamy skin on show, Saiph couldn't help but notice. *Who was she?* It was clear from the tension that lined her body that she knew exactly who, or perhaps *what,* Saiph was, which was curious in itself. This woman was someone the twins trusted. Likely not a prostitute then, but someone using their beauty just as cunningly and with as much strength as any sword Saiph could pick up.

"I don't think I've had the pleasure," Saiph purred, and Orien's eyes flashed, making her laugh deeply and flash him a quick peek at her fangs. Auren reached up from her place inside the wooden booth and tugged

Saiph down sharply. She glanced at her in surprise and took in Auren's tight jaw with bewilderment. Saiph glanced towards Orien in question, but he was too busy glaring daggers at her to answer the question in her gaze. "I'm assuming you're not here as a snack—as much as that pains me to say, because you are simply *divine*." Saiph inhaled deeply. "You smell like the outdoors, like fresh flowers and clouds."

The woman was very still, her heavily lashed eyes assessing Saiph's every move, and she decided she liked her. She was wily, this one. The woman sat back against the wall of the booth, letting her shoulders sink down as though she were relaxed, and a small smile flirted with her lips.

"Not a snack, no. I'm far too useful for that, I'm afraid."

"And much too pretty to be eaten, I suppose."

Orien was looking between them with no shortage of horror, as though he would rather die than let them converse for a second longer—this, of course, made it all the more alluring to Saiph.

Orien spoke before Saiph could say anything further. "This is Valentina." He gave no further explanation, but the possessive arm he slid around her shoulders nearly made Saiph laugh.

"I'm assuming this is your oh-so-elusive source, Orien? I'm not sure why you and your sister thought you would have so much trouble. She seems more than willing to be... caught, to me." Saiph threw Valentina a wink, and the woman grinned as if instinctively before catching the look Orien sent her way and letting it wither.

"Yes, this is Valentina and—"

Saiph didn't think, she just moved. The slight sing of steel, the taste of fear and anticipation on her tongue as it permeated the air, the man moving just a shade too close to their booth as he moved past. She shoved the man backwards and he fell into the table across the way from them, sending drinks flying and liquid pouring down to the floor.

Auren gaped at her, and Saiph's eyes got caught on the fullness of her ruined lip for a moment before she grinned savagely.

"What the fuck?" Orien roared, and the men at the table next to them shouted with him, already swinging at the would-be assassin, and Saiph laughed, her chest feeling lighter than it had in days. Regardless of the moral questions Auren had dumped on her, there was nothing that made Saiph feel quite as alive as a fight.

"My apologies, next time I'll allow you all to be stabbed to death—but I was under the impression that we were allies, for the moment, anyway. Therefore, I didn't think it would be very honourable to let you all bleed out."

"He has a knife?" Valentina asked with a little tilt to her eyebrows that said she wasn't sure whether Saiph was telling the truth, then her eyes widened comically large as she stared behind Saiph. "He has a knife!" she shouted, and then chaos truly did break loose.

The would-be assassin was a thin and weedy white man with greasy hair and sunken eyes. A man triple his size charged at him, and he disappeared beneath the man's weight. Saiph clapped as she doubled over in laughter. The men crashed into a drunken group of mortals by the bar, who all immediately shoved them backwards and dove on them in a pile. Suddenly, it seemed as though they were all fighting, regardless of allegiances.

"Is it always like this here?" Saiph asked Auren, sure that the smile on her face was probably inappropriate but unable to bring herself to care.

"I wish I could say no," Auren admitted and bit her lip. A peppery scent caught in Saiph's nose, and she wrinkled it as she glanced around and paused as her eyes fell on a man standing several tables away, staring at them.

"I think we might have trou—" A whistle sounded, and Saiph instinctively ducked, reaching for Auren and finding she'd already crouched as a blade embedded itself into the wood wall of the booth behind them and shook. "Stars, what is it with you and assassins, witch?"

Orien swore, and Valentina reached beneath her skirts and unsheathed a dagger from a cleverly hidden slit. Saiph grinned at her. "I like you more and more." Orien growled, and Saiph's laugh was lost in the ensuing melee as the brawling men drew closer, pulling more and more mortals into the fray. Saiph lost sight of the assassin and then chuckled when he popped up close enough to see her fangs, paled, and ran.

"Valentina!" Orien shouted, and Saiph turned around in time to see Valentina shove her dagger through the gut of what had to be yet another assassin that had been standing almost directly behind Saiph, but she had missed the next attacker bearing down on her. Saiph cursed colourfully and pulled *Vidi* from its glamoured sheath at her back and swung. Valentina's face became bloodless as she stared at Saiph in something akin to horror—maybe even betrayal, considering she had likely just saved Saiph from an uncomfortable encounter—and then relief as the other assassin's head fell to the floor with a wet thump behind her, sending a spray of blood over her face.

"Th-thank you," Valentina panted, and Saiph grinned.

"Well, I couldn't have another blood debt on my hands now, could I?"

Two other men stepped through the tavern's door, and Saiph scented the steel on them before they even laid eyes on her group within the crowd.

"We need to blend in," Saiph said, grabbing both Valentina and Auren by the arm and throwing them into the fight almost every patron was now involved in. Saiph barked a wild laugh as an elbow flew into her chin and snapped her head back. "Is it some kind of mortal custom to brawl every time you're in one of these establishments? If so, I approve." She slammed her fist into the face of the man closest to her and snagged an approaching woman by the hair and clunked her head into the side of the bar.

Auren was laughing as a man approached her with a lethally meaty fist, and Saiph laughed too when she spotted Valentina sneaking up behind him before leaping up onto his back with a howl like a wildcat. She clung to his neck as he spun around, and Saiph errantly kicked another drunken mortal onto the floor by their stomach as she watched. The barkeep seemed to be resigned to this ridiculousness, only raising a warning brow and tapping his hand to the blade strapped to his side when a patron got too close to the bar.

A rapid drumming sounded in Saiph's ears, and she glanced around curiously, expecting to see someone slamming their hands on the bar or a nearby table, but she could see nothing. The drums stuttered and then picked up again even faster. Warmth infused the air around her, and saliva filled Saiph's mouth. There was a cacophony of scents, rich and tangy, deep and sweet like honey. Blood flew from mouths, was knocked by noses, coated split knuckles, and beckoned on blades, and Saiph's tongue swept over her lip in longing, and then—there. The assassin from before, he'd run when he'd seen what she was, and now he approached Auren from behind, blade grasped tightly in a palm Saiph could smell was coated in sweat. She knew what she had to do, what the blood debt *demanded* that she do, and moved so that she was at his neck within one of his pounding heartbeats. Saiph blew gently and felt the heat from his skin tug at her, her fangs lengthening as she watched the pulsation of his blood. She could end this here, have her fill of this man, equalise the blood debt, and kill Auren and the rest. Saiph hesitated.

A fist flew out and caught the man in the face, and Saiph blinked at Auren as she shook her hand out and Orien moved to stand beside her.

"What are you waiting for?" Auren asked, and Saiph couldn't answer as she realised she'd missed her chance, that the witch had saved herself. Auren nodded to the man, and Saiph groaned as she saw the blood pouring from his split lip. She hauled him up to an upright position with ease and slid a hand into his greying hair, thrust his neck back, and panted. She glanced to Auren once and wasn't really sure why, but somehow felt a little relieved when she nodded in response.

Saiph didn't hesitate. Her fangs sank into the assassin's neck with no resistance, and the blood that poured into her was rich. She felt a strange stirring in her middle and then realised exactly what it was—her magick. She had been right. She could feel her magick and strength replenishing itself as the blood poured into her. With that mystery solved, Saiph relaxed slightly, letting the man fall to the ground with his hand clasped over his throat before she could drain him completely. Already her control was improving, and Auren gave her another nod, as though she approved. There was something else in her eyes, a question, and Saiph stepped forward, curious for an insight into the witch's mind when Orien emerged from nowhere, dragging Valentina behind him, and Auren's mouth snapped shut.

The room had mostly emptied at some point, likely while Saiph was fangs-deep in the assassin that was currently attempting to crawl towards the door. The innkeeper sighed as he came out from behind the bar and surveyed the mess.

"This is going to take an age to clear up."

"I'm afraid it might take a little longer," Saiph said as she strode towards the half-dead man and plucked him up, shoving him into a chair that Auren procured. Their eyes met for a moment, and Saiph knew that in that moment they were perfectly in sync. "Close the bar. This might get messy."

CHAPTER EIGHTEEN
AUREN

THIS WAS NOT HOW AUREN HAD IMAGINED THIS evening going. Perhaps that had been foolish—things did so often end with blood where Saiph was involved —though admittedly, the same could likely be said of Auren too.

Orien's absence was like a tangible thing in the caves. It seemed quieter without his laugh, and the air was too light without him by her side. It was a necessary evil for him to remain in Eloria, but she didn't have to like it—even if it did give her more time to work on the plan she had concocted that Ren had vetoed. He felt that seducing the enemy, and the heir to throne of the Kingdom of Stars no less, was a spectacularly bad idea. Actually, if she recalled correctly, his exact phrasing had been: "Are you *fucking insane?*"

Despite all that, she'd had a lot of fun tonight. There was nothing as invigorating as a bar fight, and tonight's had been spectacular. She'd been having it a lot, she realised—fun. The heir was nothing at all like she'd anticipated, and they had some sort of connection through the blood debt that Auren wasn't sure what to make of. Perhaps she could use it to her advantage. Saiph was proving unusually resilient to her charms, even with the unfamiliar bloodlust she'd been experiencing since coming to Somnium—though the threat Saiph's mother posed would be enough to ruin the mood for anyone.

Yet... there had been the long looks, the nips of flirtation, and the heat that grew under Auren's skin whenever the star was close by... The game of seduction they'd played in the rooms above this very bar. It was possible this *longing* was one-sided, but still, she hoped. She'd known it was the right thing for duty's sake that she should attempt to unify their kingdoms by seducing the heir, to follow in her father's footsteps and make peace rather than more war, she just hadn't realised that she might actually *want* to seduce her.

Saiph stood in front of the only assassin they'd left alive after the brawl, her long legs wide-spread and her hands on her narrow hips. One of the swords at her back was lightly bloodied, and Auren smirked, remembering Valentina's face when Saiph had decapitated that assassin over the top of her head. Her fangs were out, small but able to do a lot of damage, and the man now tied to one of the high-backed wooden chairs looked as if he were fully aware of that fact. A widening stain spread over his crotch, and Saiph huffed in disgust. Auren bit her tongue so as not to react—her senses were not quite as good as Saiph's, but unfortunately she could smell the evidence of the man's fear just fine.

Valentina stood at the bar, murmuring to the barkeep about the mess and had he seen that assassin she'd gutted? Auren stifled a laugh at the amused look on Orien's face as he undoubtedly eavesdropped too. Auren refocused on Saiph as she leaned in and pressed a hand onto the armrests either side of the captive. He shuddered, cringing away from Saiph in desperation as he kept his eyes on her fangs.

"Please," he said, voice cracking and fresh sweat breaking out along his forehead. "I was just going off orders. I'll leave—I—nobody has to know——"

Saiph cut him off, leaning in closer, but Auren analysed the man's face, the way he scanned Saiph's face in not only fear but *hope*—as though he thought appealing to her was the best way out of this. But why?

"Do you know who I am?" Saiph breathed, letting a fang scrape tauntingly down the pulse beating frantically in the man's neck, and a stab of envy and *want* shot through her.

Valentina paled slightly as she turned to watch but stayed where she was. Auren knew it was conflicting for her, to see the raw evidence of what her and Orien were, what the *stars* were—but she was soul bonded to Auren's brother, so she'd better get used to it.

The man nodded, his hair shaking with the force as

he hurried to answer, and Auren saw the surprise flash across Saiph's face, there and gone in half a heartbeat. Whatever it was that this man hid, Saiph was unaware of it too. Hadn't expected him to recognise her so easily.

"Then why are you here?" Saiph said, leaning back and peering at the man's face, the picture of ease. She had nothing to fear. She could move ten-times faster than the mortal man, even if he could escape the rope binding his hands and feet to the chair. Besides which, Auren would—

She would, what? Save the life of her enemy? Again? *Yes,* she reasoned slowly, it would be hard to unite their kingdoms by marrying an heir who was dead. Auren hadn't given her actions too much thought when she had been in the smuggler's tunnel with Saiph—it certainly hadn't been part of the plan to be captured— but once she was there, all she knew was that if she wanted her plan to work, she needed the heir in her debt. After that, Orien couldn't really argue against her plan—the blood debt had fallen right into their laps. Sometimes the Fates made your choice for you.

The man's eyes flicked to Auren and then back to Saiph. "She shouldn't have been allowed to escape. They just told us to kill the woman with the scar on her mouth, to take care of the problem before..."

"Before?" Orien's eyes were as cold as the tips of his fingers, and Auren squeezed his hand as she caught hold of him before he could reach the assassin. They needed more information, and if Ren got his hands on him, they'd likely be left guessing. She understood. The idea of those filthy excuses for men *allowing* her to do anything was as laughable as it was enraging, but Auren pushed back the tingling in her gums and focused.

The assassin kept glancing at Saiph as if looking for direction, and Auren wanted to laugh when the heir pasted the fakest-looking pleasant smile on her face and hissed, "Tell my friends here what they want to know."

Friends. It was a slight step-up from the *allies* Saiph had quoted earlier, and Auren hid a grimace at Ren's look of amusement. Auren needed to take things up a notch, clearly, if Saiph was only just willing to categorise them as such. The captive gave a shaky nod, as if relieved by Saiph's words.

"They needed to cover it up before the queen found out."

The cogs in Auren's brain were turning but too slowly, and Orien shook his head in apparent disgust. "The queen would never —"

"And what about me?" Saiph said. It was a voice Auren had never heard her use before. Quiet, no doubt deadly, but there was something buried underneath like if Auren tugged just a little, Saiph might unravel in front of her. "I was captured too. Why are they not also hunting me?"

The assassin looked appalled, mouth dropping open in horror and eyes widening in a way that had to be painful. "You should never have been there, Highness, and they would never hurt *you!*"

It clicked, and Auren let out a groan. Orien's eyes peered at her in concern, and she swallowed, but Saiph spoke before she could.

"I don't think," Saiph said slowly as she stood and moved away from the shivering man, "that *your* queen is the one they're claiming to work for, witch."

Orien's mouth dropped open, and he shook his head. "You don't think—"

Saiph nodded grimly. "I think they're working for mine."

Auren knew the exact moment that Ren lost his temper. A cool rush of air brushed against her, and her hand snapped out to catch his arm before he could leap.

"Did you know about this?" he snarled at Saiph, his fists clenched so tightly that Auren winced imagining what that grip would have done to the heir.

"Of course not, you fool. Why would I agree to hunt down these bastards and risk my mother's wrath in this deal if I'd known she had any hand in it?" For her part, Saiph looked calm, only the slight tightening of her dark eyes betraying the hit to her pride. Auren squeezed Orien's arm to the point of bruising, and he hissed in pain as he turned his glare on her. She didn't care. Accusing someone of betrayal was *not* a good way to propose.

"Traitor," the assassin gasped, a little slow on the

uptake, but his face had drained of all colour as he realised what he'd done and stared up at Saiph.

"Now, now," Saiph hissed, looming back over him. "It's not nice to call people names."

Auren caught the flash of a knife before Saiph did and cried out a warning as the man's bindings fell loose. He jumped up, and Saiph fell back. Auren wasn't sure why until she saw the blade sticking out of her chest and shouted in rage. Star-spun steel, it had to be in order to have pierced the skin of a star.

The room bled red as the assassin jumped at her. *She isn't dead. She's a fucking star, nearly impossible to kill. She's not dead.* Panic churned through her veins, but it wasn't enough to counteract the pure rage that flooded her as the assassin stepped forward and brandished another knife in her direction.

Auren laughed as she beckoned him forward, knocking Orien back with a blast of magic that forced him to Valentina's side. One slash, two, Auren stepped nimbly to the side underneath his blade before catching his arm from beneath and snapping it at the elbow.

Saiph's brief groan of pain called her attention away. It was low, and without her enhanced hearing, Auren likely wouldn't have heard it, but somehow it covered the scream of the assassin as he gripped his broken arm. Her rage burned hotter as she lost herself in the sensations of the room, the tang of blood and sweat, Saiph's anger and embarrassment clouding the air and making Auren's fingers ache with the need to heal, to rage. Orien was calling her name, wrapped in a ring of fire with Valentina that she couldn't remember deciding to conjure. She knew why he was worried and paused to spare him a glance. She was in control, mostly. It wasn't like before. She'd trained a lot since that day in the Forest for exactly that reason. She would never again lose herself completely to the magick, would never again allow someone she loved to be hurt—especially not by her own hand.

Auren reached down and pulled the assassin up carelessly from where he'd crumpled to the floor. He'd vomited, and she neatly dodged the pile as she dragged him to Saiph by the arm that dangled uselessly at his side while he howled. She bent down to whisper in his ear, knowing full well that Saiph would be able to hear them if she chose. "You stabbed someone under *my* protection. Apologise." The man whimpered, but his mouth remained shut. Auren brutally squeezed his arm and snarled until his face was white with pain and his body shook. Saiph's eyes had lifted, the knife removed from her chest and dripping blood onto the floor. Sweat dotted her hairline and caught in her long hair like small gemstones, glinting against the silvery strands. "*Apologise.*"

Auren knew she should be more careful, shouldn't give away too much of her magickal skill or her strength, not when Saiph's allegiances were so precarious. But the heir's dark eyes were like pitch on Auren's, and the sight of her fangs, wet and gleaming behind her full mouth, sent heat cascading through her, pulling her away from the room in a daze. The crackling of her flames faded away, and the frantic *thump-thump-thump* of the heart beating in the man's chest only stoked her bloodlust.

Saiph blinked her dark eyes, accepting Auren's offering, and she found herself moving closer until she could count each of the long, white eyelashes that surrounded Saiph's eyes, basking in the glow her body cast off. She swung the man around to face her, longing to sink her fangs and make this filth *scream*. But she couldn't give in to the rage that still lurked in her bones, not like that. Instead, she pulled him close and tucked his head beneath her chin, looked down at Saiph with her own nod, and then swiftly dug her hands into his throat.

Auren tore across in a deep slash that half-satiated the animalistic need to protect that he had created when he had slammed the dagger up to the hilt into the heir's chest. Blood sprayed out from between her fingers in an arc, and faintly Auren heard the barkeep sigh, had nearly forgotten he was here bearing witness to this. Then her eyes were back on Saiph's as she finally leaned down and drank before grimacing. "Not enough."

The assassin's knife still sat in the palm of her hand, bloodied, and Saiph's glamour had slipped a little as all her energy was redirected to healing herself. She knelt on the floor at Auren's feet, and a new thrill swept through her, the heir on her knees—finally. Yet, it wasn't where Saiph belonged.

The man groaned, his face pale, and rage swept through her so absolutely that she knew Orien sensed it as he moved toward them. Before he could reach them, Auren leaned down, her voice guttural and unlike her own as she pressed her hand to the man's chest. "You should have apologised." Then she shoved her hand through to his still-beating heart, clasping it in her fingers and squeezing wetly before recoiling her arm in a snap and holding her offering out to the star as the strange rage finally retreated. "*Seren.*"

Saiph took it, her eyes a little wide, before burning it to ashes in a wash of silvery blue flames that probably cost her dearly given the blood she had already lost. She was graceful as she stood, always so graceful, and her long-fingered hand was light and glowing in Auren's. On her feet, Saiph raised her head, tension radiating out from her lithe body.

"Why do you insist on calling me that? *Seren?*"

It was not what Auren had been expecting her to say, and she bit her lip to hide her surprise. Blood had dyed the ends of Saiph's hair red, but her eyes were steady on Auren's once more. "It means silver."

Saiph nodded and fingered a bloodied piece of her hair. "Original."

Auren let loose the small laugh that was bubbling up inside. *She wasn't dead.* "Not for your hair, though it's remarkable, as I'm sure you well know."

Now Saiph's interest seemed truly piqued. Her eyes roved Auren's face and dropped to her mouth, making Auren's stomach tighten.

"Why?" Saiph asked bluntly. Auren knew what she was asking but feigned ignorance, choosing instead to answer the question of her nickname rather than look too closely at what had prompted her to avenge Saiph's honour in such a graphic manner. Mostly because she herself wasn't sure. It was as though a monster made only of rage and panic had flooded her body, begging her to *protect, protect, protect,* until that sensation had felt more real to her than anything else in the room—save the infuriating woman now standing opposite her.

"Because the first time I saw you, the *real* you, you were like a blade flashing in the dark as you cut those men down and painted yourself in their blood. It left an impression."

"Surely *red* would make more sense then," Orien called from the other side of the room and was largely ignored by the both of them.

Saiph took one step closer, and Auren's breath caught in her throat at the naked *want* in her eyes.

"Saiph I—"

Her mouth was silenced by Saiph's descending and covering her own, warm and hard, almost punishing as it nipped at her. It felt like all of the pieces inside her fell together, blending in a way that left only blissful desire humming in her mind as heat built in her core and she tasted Saiph's blood on her tongue. Auren's bloodied hands moved up, sliding through Saiph's hair and marvelling at the softness as Saiph's lips pressed harder against her. She sank her teeth into Auren's bottom lip, and Auren let out a hiss of both pain and pleasure. Saiph drew back, her dark eyes questioning as she licked away the small hurt. It would be a risk. It was possible Saiph would be able to taste the secrets Auren had been keeping... but the pros outweighed the cons. She needed to show the heir that what she felt went beyond allies, beyond friends, beyond the debt that had forced them together. She needed to show her she trusted her and Auren found, to her surprise, that she actually did. Saiph had started to move away when Auren gave her a small nod, stepping closer, and Orien hissed a warning as Saiph struck.

CHAPTER NINETEEN
SAIPH

Auren's blood was like nothing Saiph had ever tasted before. Admittedly, Saiph's experience was limited, but the men she had tasted had been... watery, weak, and she hadn't even known it until her fangs had sunk into the skin of the queen's guard. It was a riot of flavour sending warmth burning through Saiph's body, as though Auren's flames could burn their way through her and brand her as its own. Maybe it was the magic in Auren's soul, but Saiph felt drunk, like she was drinking whiskey wrapped in starfire, speeding through her, igniting her soul.

Orien was shouting somewhere, and dimly Saiph wondered if Auren's circle of flames had fallen yet—if not, that was a claim to both serious power and skill if Auren could give her power to Saiph like this and yet still maintain perfect control of the fire in the corner. Auren's hands reached out, and Saiph tensed, but

Auren only pulled her closer, tilted her head a little further up to give Saiph better access, and gave a loud moan that sent an entirely different sensation shooting through her.

The wound that had been open and bloody on her chest moments ago was now a pearlescent white as new skin formed and shone in the lantern light. Saiph drew back, and Auren mumbled a protest as she swayed on her feet. Saiph caught Auren against her body, trying to ignore the softness of her curves pressed so tightly against her and frowned at herself when she realised her hands were tangled in the shining mass of Auren's light brown hair. This was not the distance she had been hoping to maintain after their tryst, but when your enemy kills for you, offers up the heart of your attacker for you to claim—at what point do you admit that perhaps they are foe no longer?

Orien whipped his sister away as he rushed to her side, sliding in between them, not quite shoving Saiph away but not exactly being gentle either, and a low snarl built in her throat. Orien glanced at her in surprise, and Saiph cut the sound off—what was wrong with her? Was this a reaction to the blood? Valentina came towards them, looking hesitant, and Saiph wanted to grin at the blood that still speckled her face from the earlier brawl, but all she could manage was that same snarl of warning, and Orien echoed it when he saw it directed at Valentina. In the end, it was the barkeep who intervened, keeping well away but speaking so sharply that it cut through the strange fog impeding on Saiph's emotions.

"Enough. You've caused quite enough damage for one night, thank you. I suggest you go to bed and emerge with better attitudes come dawn." With one last serious look, he stomped off towards a door that led to the rooms they were expected to settle in for tonight before they sprung their trap tomorrow.

Orien hustled Valentina and a highly groggy Auren to the same door, and Auren whimpered as they passed Saiph, reaching out with one hand and letting it drop when Saiph didn't respond. Whatever it was that had just happened after drinking Auren's blood, no matter how good it felt, she wouldn't be doing it again. Not until she knew what it meant, not until she knew for sure that Auren could be... not an enemy, and have them both survive.

Saiph sat down heavily after righting a fallen chair. In truth, from everything she'd observed in the caves and on earth... the mortals did not seem like the villains that the history of the Kingdom of the Stars painted them to be. That her mother had claimed. Generally, the people who win the war are usually the ones better off, but most of the people Saiph had seen barely had food, let alone riches.

She loved her people and her kingdom, but what did it make her if she was so ready to further destroy those living here for... what, exactly? A throne that meant nothing with nobody to sit on it? And Saiph had truly found no evidence of the queen's existence so far. This war the stars seemed determined to wage on the mortals seemed more and more ridiculous the longer Saiph spent on their plane.

But the truth of the matter was that Saiph was not in charge. Her mother was, and as long as that was the case, it mattered very little whether or not Saiph approved—she was heir to a throne she wouldn't inherit for more years than the human lifespan contained. A hint of despair filled her as she considered Auren, nothing more than bone and dust while Saiph lived on.

There was little love lost between Saiph and her mother. Saiph wanted what was best for her people— which she now realised should have always included the mortals—and her mother wanted power. The lengths that Queen Fallon would go to ensure she kept her throne now seemed unsettling, no longer the acts of a fit ruler and more that of a power-hungry villain. She had *trained the weakness out of her* at a young age, testing her with darkness and magic and earth—all in the name of strengthening her, of protecting the crown and ensuring she was safe from the mortals who would seek to hurt her, torture her. Yet, the only pain Saiph had suffered on the mortal plane was at the hands of the men working on her mother's behalf.

"MOTHER! Please! You cannot leave us here, don't leave us here! Mother!" Saiph's voice reverberated around her strangely. It was

not something she had ever experienced before, the way a voice could be trapped and muffled. Lost entirely to dirt until you couldn't remember if you ever had a voice at all. The flaming torch grew farther away with her mother's unfaltering steps, and still Saiph screamed, begged, gripping her hair as the loss of light wracked through her, until the light turned a corner and absolute darkness fell.

"Why don't you care?" she had screamed at her twin, and Vala blinked her amber eyes solemnly, placing a soothing hand on Saiph's where she was frantically burying her hands into the dirt floor over and over. They were both barefoot, having been dragged out of bed and brought to this place where nobody could hear them scream. Would she leave them to die down here?

"I do care, but I also know that she does not." Vala's words allowed a small bit of reason to worm its way into Saiph's head, and when Vala tugged on her hands again, Saiph relinquished the dirt.

"She wants to make us strong," Saiph said hesitantly, the momentary calm allowing her night vision to kick in and see her sister's dirt-smudged face opposite her own.

"She wants to make us hers," Vala corrected, and Saiph frowned—didn't they already belong to their mother? Vala could obviously see this thought passing across Saiph's face because she frowned back. "We belong to nobody but ourselves, Saiph."

The words settled inside her, feeling surprisingly right, and Saiph huddled closer to Vala as they waited for their mother's return.

· · ·

THAT HADN'T BEEN the only time her mother had locked her beneath the earth, either to test her or punish her, sometimes with Vala and oftentimes without once she realised Vala was key to keeping Saiph calm under there. She had been seven that first time she'd been shoved below ground, cut off from the starlight that kept their natures fed on the surface—the third time she'd visited the cage beneath the earth had been the first time her fangs had appeared, and her mother had thrashed her soundly when she'd been unable to retract them when she'd come to release them from below.

Saiph let a deep breath rush out of her and stood. She felt stiff from sitting still for too long and absolutely wired from Auren's blood when she would have expected exhaustion from the grave wound. It wouldn't have killed her—her kind were a lot tougher than that—but it would have taken a long time to heal without either the pure starlight they had back home, or as she now knew, blood. Powerful blood.

Her chest felt oddly warm, and she rubbed at it absently as she set about righting spilled chairs and mopping thrown drinks. There were copious splashes of blood everywhere, on the exposed brick walls that stood between the wood panels, the insides of drinking booths, dripping down the lanterns that held the fires lighting up the room. She cleaned it all and leaned heavily against the bar when she was done. It had seemed only fair. That had been the second brawl she'd started in this establishment.

She reached behind the bar and poured herself a measure of whiskey straight into her mouth and didn't startle when the barkeep said from the entryway, "Thank you."

A smile curled over her mouth, and she let it linger for a second before taking a second swig of whiskey, placing the bottle back behind the bar and pushing away to the room she had waiting above. He muttered something about germs as she made her way past, but Saiph only smirked.

"I won't tell if you don't—consider it cleaning tax."

"For a mess you made?"

"Well, it wasn't just me."

The barkeep huffed a laugh, and Saiph smiled as she pushed through the door and made her way up the stairs. She bit down on her own amusement as she passed what had to be Orien and Valentina's room judging by the sounds coming from inside. Sometimes her sensitive hearing was more a curse than a blessing.

Her room was the same one she and Auren had shared before, and she wondered at how often they got out of the caves to stay here—considering the room still smelled like them, Saiph was sure nobody else had been there since.

It was sparse but practically royal in there compared to the caves—though in fact, Saiph didn't mind it as much as she'd thought she would. She had never been one to care about *things*, save for her swords. She shucked them off and placed them on a wooden chair that had been set by the window and slid off her boots and sturdy trousers too. She was mid-way through unlacing the ties on her shirt when the bed rustled, and her muscles froze. The smell of earth and heat and spice washed over her, and Saiph unconsciously relaxed. Auren. She'd known the witch would likely be in here, but under the cover of true night, her presence felt electric, nonetheless.

She was letting herself get sloppy to not have sensed she was in here from the moment Saiph stepped in. *Tired*, she reasoned. It had been a very long day—the trip through the Forest that afternoon now felt like a lifetime ago, which was no small feat for a star. In fact, with Auren, it often felt like Saiph was more aware of the minutes than usual as they passed. She drew Saiph into the moment so that all she could think about was her. It was only in her absence that time seemed to resume its normal pace. It must be hard, Saiph realised, to be a mortal and be so aware of death looming around every corner, getting closer with each breath.

Her footsteps barely made a sound as Saiph moved closer to the double bed, the laces from her top dangling loosely and tickling her arms when she walked, yet Auren stirred, murmured her name.

"Is there a reason you're in my bed again, witch?" Saiph asked softly. Was this about the kiss? Had she given the impression that she wanted a repeat of that and the other things that had transpired last time they were here?

She'd been trying not to think about it, the way it

had scorched her and the way all she could taste even now was Auren's lips on hers—more potent, even, than her blood. It was a dangerous game to play, for too many reasons.

"Yours, mine, they are one and the same." Auren sighed, and confusion made Saiph blink. Auren's hair was fanned across one pillow, her face tilted upwards to meet Saiph's gaze even as her eyes remained closed. One long leg had escaped the white sheets and was tangled in a way that made Saiph's stomach lurch as she followed the gleam of Auren's skin from her foot to the curve of her hip and up, over her waist—

"Are you *naked?*" It had slipped out before Saiph could rein it in, and the witch's full mouth smirked as her golden eyes finally fluttered open.

"You say that with such outrage, though you were about to do the same thing, no?"

Saiph glanced down—her own bare skin had been forgotten in her shock—and rolled her eyes. Auren had seen far more of her regularly in the bathing chamber, but being in bed with her... bare once more to Saiph's touch—

Her fangs throbbed in time with a pulse that was far lower, and Saiph swallowed dryly.

"Yes, well, I hadn't realised I was to have company," was all she could reply.

Auren gave a low laugh that rubbed along Saiph's skin, curling invitingly, and Saiph moved forward another step. "*Liar.* Unfortunately, *seren,* unlike your mother, we do not have endless amounts of gold. So

I'm afraid these are the sleeping arrangements, but it's only for one more night."

She'd known, Saiph thought in wonder. Auren had known that Saiph was to share her bed, and yet she had still stripped bare and curled herself in their sheets, and some part of her delighted in that fact. Perhaps she did not regret what had happened after all.

Only for one night. Saiph was acutely aware of each of her breaths and how the cool air flicked across her sensitive skin, but she ignored it. She could share a bed with the witch one more time.

The shirt hit the pile of clothes on the chair, and Saiph sank into the bed on the opposite side of Auren. The sheets were warm, and every time the bed jostled a little with Auren's movements, Saiph's heart fumbled. Needles prickled under her skin, like her traitorous body was begging her to reach out, to slide a little closer. Saiph's leg moved, just a fraction, and Auren's heart beat harder. Was it possible that Auren wanted whatever it was that Saiph did too? The warmth in her chest grew at the thought, a pleased hum trying to escape her lips that Saiph shoved back down. This was irrational. Her mother would kill her if she discovered Saiph had broken the law and fucked a mortal. Worse, she would kill Auren.

Heat rose in her face, and she bit her lip to stall the curse that wanted to explode out of her. When had *that* happened? When had the thought of Auren's death come to scare her more than that of her own? She felt lost inside her own skin, drowning in want and desire and hissing as it fought against duty and caution.

Only for one night. Tomorrow this could all be over. They would meet the smugglers and kill them, and the timelines between the plane of the Kingdom of Stars and the mortal plane would merge once more. The only way out of the blood debt was to save Auren's life, or to complete the given task of hunting and killing those responsible for their kidnapping and the disappearance of the magick users. Given that Saiph's mother was responsible, she would need to save Auren's life to nullify the deal—and she would only have a very small window to do it before her mother would be able to see Somnium again and discover the truth of Saiph's crimes, which would likely spell the death of them all.

Either way, tomorrow would bring either Auren's death or her own. Suddenly there wasn't enough air in her lungs. Her eyes burned, and her fists clenched. Her relationship with her mother was complicated and what she felt for Auren was... not. Could she have this moment, even knowing that tomorrow, Saiph would likely have to kill her or face losing everything?

Saiph rolled on her side and found Auren's eyes already on her face, solemn in the dark.

"Auren, I—"

"You're still going to pick her, aren't you? Even after everything you've seen here. You know she'll kill us all, Saiph."

She grit her teeth against the dampness she could

feel in her eyes, blinking rapidly as she met Auren's steady gaze. "What else can I do? She is the queen, and no matter what you or I think of her, I cannot just…"

Auren bit her bottom lip, and Saiph couldn't pull her gaze away. "Nobody is asking you to kill her." The room fell silent, only the sound of their breaths and hearts disturbing the stillness. "We know about the timeline, the way it diverges. Tomorrow you will have to make your choice."

Saiph's eyes flared wide, though she supposed she couldn't be too surprised—Auren was intelligent, and hadn't Saiph herself even thought that the humans had themselves a guide to the timeline with their chart of the attacks? Saiph rolled away and onto her back and kept her eyes on the ceiling, letting out a deep breath as she replied, "There never has been a choice for me. Either I do as she expects and kill you and your queen, for you are human and I am a star. Or I save you, and she kills us both. Or I fail to save you and the blood debt kills me anyway. There is no good way out of this. If my mother suspects our… agreement, she will kill me, and likely you as well, once she's tortured you for information on the heir."

Auren's hand found Saiph's in the darkness and squeezed it tightly. "Or we fight—for each other, for the kingdoms we are sworn to protect. There are… things, that you don't know and I cannot tell you. But she is only as powerful as you let her be, Saiph."

Saiph pushed away the emotions building in her

chest, keeping her voice as unaffected as possible as she said, "I cannot promise you anything, *ignis cordis mei*. You should not underestimate her."

Auren's hand slipped away. "You underestimate yourself. And me."

CHAPTER TWENTY
SAIPH

THEY SLEPT FOR MOST OF THE DAY AND AWOKE AS THE sun began to set. The sheets had been cold to the touch by the time Saiph had risen and made her way to the small bathing chamber adjacent to their room. Auren's scent still lingered on the air, grabbing Saiph's heart in a fist as she recalled their whispered conversation last night.

Nobody's asking you to kill her. But were they not? The witch was delusional if she thought they could escape from this without spilling Queen Fallon's blood. But was it worth it? To commit the same sins as her mother, allegedly, and become a kin-killer if it saved Kara? Auren? Countless other mortals? Was it what was best for both the kingdoms Saiph would be set to rule over?

She thought she knew the answer, and it terrified her. Fear wasn't an emotion she was accustomed with, not for a long time. It had been so soundly beaten out of her that she was surprised to feel its sting that evening as they bickered over tankards of ale.

"*Enough*, Ren! Saiph saved my life last night and she's the most logical choice as bait. I trust her." Valentina's dark eyes flashed with menace, and Saiph felt a little impressed as Orien was reduced to silence. Auren, however, showed no such signs of cowing.

"She's too much of a giveaway. Saiph can't keep her fangs hidden for two chimes, let alone long enough for us to trail the smuggler back to their base."

Valentina shook her head. "They're actively hunting for you, Auren. They might recognise Orien from his contact with me, and I'm the one who spoke to the smuggler—it has to be her."

The twins had grumbled before reluctantly acquiescing, and Valentina held a smug expression on her face as they checked their weapons one final time before leaving. The unfamiliar weight of two additional daggers strapped to her thighs jolted Saiph when she walked. She was used to having only her swords and her magick and maybe a knife in her boot, so this felt slightly overzealous—but if it made the mortals feel better, then she would wear them.

As soon as they'd left the tavern, Saiph had pulled her hood up. Auren had been right, her bright silver hair was a dead giveaway, and she intended to give their enemies no easy advantages. The night was dark and still. The sunlight faded out early at this time of the year apparently, and Saiph was grateful as it aided their plans.

The streets were long and winding, and the small wood and brick houses mostly hid them from view. At the very least, it cut off the wind, and Saiph knew Valentina was grateful when she huddled down further into her cloak.

The twins seemed unaffected by the cold, their footsteps practically silent as they led the way to the town square. They had decided to take up positions in the alleyways flanking the bell tower, but Saiph could hear Orien and Valentina arguing about where she was to be during all of this.

"If things go badly, you need to be out of the way so you can run and tell Raze what happened. I can't be focused on you when we need to have our attention focused on Saiph."

Valentina's words held no small amount of bite when she finally relented. "Fine. But if it looks like you need my help, I won't sit by in safety."

Orien sounded ready to protest again when they drew close to the centre of town, and Auren silenced them with a wave of her hand.

"You know what to do," Auren said to Saiph, and she nodded once before moving out towards the bell tower by herself. It truly was extraordinary what the mortals had managed to build—everything in the Kingdom of Stars ran off of starlight, and while the mortals had mastered running water, they didn't yet have the technology to master light. Though, she supposed it was hard to progress when you constantly had to rebuild.

The bell tolled ten chimes, and the sound seemed to vibrate through Saiph's skull and teeth. It was time.

"Was it enough?"

Auren didn't have to ask what Orien was talking about as they moved to the alley just south of the bell tower, doing well to keep to the shadows and their voices low. They both knew how important tonight was as the timelines re-converged—especially now they knew Fallon was the one masterminding the kidnappings, whether out of sadistic malice or to weaken Auren's court, she didn't yet know.

Saiph had a choice to make, and Auren wasn't sure it would be the one she hoped.

Auren shook her head. She knew she looked unusually pale and washed out with dark circles around her eyes, but it had been hard to sleep knowing that today could very well spell the deaths of more than one of them. "I don't know what she'll choose, Ren. Maybe I didn't do enough… She wants to help us, I know it. She just doesn't want to kill her mother to do it."

Orien steadied her with one hand to her shoulder. "You did everything you could. It's up to her now. As long as that blood debt is in place, she can't hurt you, even if her mother screams for it."

"That's what scares me."

"But you'll be safe."

"I would rather be dead than safe if her mother kills her to get to me, Ren."

He stared at her, shocked. "Auren, don't be ridiculous! You may have come to care for the heir, but she is not worth sacrificing everything we've worked for—"

"She is my mate," Auren said, and the breath left him even as the words made something both break and rejoice inside her. Auren let out a quiet and desolate laugh in response to his horror. "The Fates are cruel indeed, brother. I felt it last night, as soon as she bit me. After I'd tasted her blood on my tongue, it just clicked—the connection we have, the attraction. I felt so *torn* for actually wanting someone who had hurt so many of our people, whether directly or not, my duty or not, and all along, she was my mate."

Orien licked his lips, and she knew that he, like her, was weighing up what this new information meant for them. It was possibly the best and worst thing that could have happened. A mate-bond all but guaranteed Auren's safety, as one mate would never attack the other. But if things went wrong, even if they managed to kill Fallon, Auren could never raise her hand to Saiph. "Do you think she knows?"

Auren bit her lip and looked up to the sky as a tear trickled down her face and was brutally wiped away. "Stars, I hope not." It would only make things harder for them both, to have found this gift from the universe, only to watch one or the other die.

"The timelines could merge again at any moment. With any luck, *she* won't notice us unless we use our magick—"

Auren interrupted him with a shake of her head. "She'll be looking for Saiph, and Saiph…"

"Is with us." Orien sighed, scrubbing a hand across his forehead. "That doesn't mean she'll recognise us." Auren looked at him like he was an idiot, a wry frown twisting her mouth, and he shook his head. "You're right, Fates know given our luck, one of us is probably the spitting image of our mother or Myrinn."

Auren laughed quietly, and Orien cupped her cheek before letting go to move to the opposite alley but stilled as Auren caught his forearm. "Something doesn't feel right."

Auren's instincts were usually impeccable, and as she let her senses stretch out further, she knew her brother would be doing the same. She normally kept them reined in so as not to be overwhelmed—a lesson she'd learned early on lest every smell on the air distract her. A cacophony of drumming surrounded them, sounding from alleys and rooftops, and Orien swore at the same time as her—heartbeats, more than she could count.

Orien tapped his ear meaningfully, and she nodded grimly.

"They must never have believed Valentina—"

"We're surrounded."

Auren spun around at his words, her eyes searching out her mate, waiting at the bell tower and preparing to follow a heavy-set man into the darkness when Auren said her name. It was quiet enough that only someone with senses as good as Saiph's would hear. "*Seren*, they were waiting for us. Fight."

The man turned to look at Saiph when she tensed, and Auren would have laughed if the timing were less inappropriate as Saiph flashed her fangs, making the man gasp.

"Surprise," she hissed and gutted him so swiftly even Auren's eyes had trouble tracking the movement. She had acted immediately and without question. Saiph trusted them—they just needed to get her mother out of the way.

As soon as the man slumped over, there was a great roar as men poured from between the buildings and rappelled from the top of roofs. Auren heard Saiph cackling wildly and spared her a quick grin as she flashed past and took off the head of a smuggler still reaching for his blade.

Saiph had shed her cloak and pulled her sword so quickly it had felt like Auren had only blinked before she was a blur of silver. Her hair darted against the darkness, and her blade quickly became soaked in red as she spun. Heads fell around her, and Auren supposed old habits died hard. Generally decapitation was the best way to kill a star, and it seemed Saiph was taking no chances.

More men seemed to be spilling from the streets closest to them, and Auren felt a stab of horror at their mass—Queen Fallon had recruited herself a veritable army of mortals, all by giving them the gold they needed for the food and shelter they wanted from a problem she had perpetuated. It was smart, she admitted begrudgingly, but it meant a great deal of blood would be spilled here before any progress could be made towards Auren reclaiming her throne.

Though, at least it was unlikely they would have to hunt down any remaining smugglers. They seemed to be there in full force tonight. Somehow, they'd known who would be waiting for them tonight.

CHAPTER TWENTY-ONE

ORIEN

ORIEN'S HANDS QUICKLY BECAME SLICK WITH BLOOD, but there were so many of them that as soon as one smuggler fell, another quickly replaced them. His blade sliced at a throat and he just managed to catch another before it could gut him, dispatching the mortal quickly. The hardest part was that he couldn't use his powers. His speed and strength would have been of great assistance but would have been a dead giveaway to Saiph that all was not what it seemed. Plus, they were trying to keep the queen's attention away from them for as long as they could, and using his magick would be like a beacon, practically begging her to take a shot.

A light, floral scent tickled his nose, and he swore. Valentina. He supposed the chances of her seeing what was happening and choosing to remain in safety were very unlikely. He wasn't surprised when the man in front of him grunted, looking down in pain and surprise at the blade that jutted out of his stomach as

Orien's mate gutted him. Valentina peered over the mortal's shoulder at him and quirked a small smile. "You didn't think I was going to let you have all the fun, did you?"

"I had hoped," Orien said dryly before they moved back-to-back amidst a mob of men and women, all clamouring to end them.

There was an ever-widening circle around Saiph and Auren, the ground beneath them soaked red and littered with heads. Valentina caught sight of it and blanched.

"Fuck. They don't do things in halves," she panted, and Orien laughed as he caught a thrown blade aimed at his chest and launched it back at its owner. It gave a satisfying *thunk* as it made contact and the woman fell. There had to be over a hundred humans now, pressed so tightly into the town square that they could barely move, which was proving useful as they couldn't have kept them all back from rushing them at once.

Orien suspected Saiph was keeping her magic under wraps for the same reason he and Auren were— her mother. The crowd surged forwards, and Orien struggled to maintain his footing on the slick ground. Valentina stumbled, and he reached for her clumsily. His hand grasped at air and was quickly crushed in the throng as she was ripped away from him. Her brown hair fluttered briefly, just a few steps ahead of him, and panic and frantic need tore into him as he heard her shout. The crowd writhed, and the men in front of him laughed as he cut them down, caring only for reaching her, using his hands to shove into chests and rip out hearts as he ploughed into the mass of people.

"Valentina!" He called for her over and over as he hunted, power flowing through him, and his breath crystalised in front of his face as his rage and panic surmounted. Stars, if they'd just solidified the bond, she would have been stronger. He could have protected her better. *Stars.*

There was no response to his calls. He tried to listen for her heart—a sound he would know anywhere —but it was impossible with so many others beating. He was happy to remove that obstacle though. *Valentina, Valentina,* Orien roared as ice spilled through his veins. His thoughts were caught on her name, and he breathed deeply, hoping to catch her scent amidst the iron tang of blood and the heaviness of the mud that splattered all of them. Nothing. Like she had never been there.

He couldn't even feel the nicks and cuts the mortals landed as he pushed through them. He was only half-star, so while his skin was more resilient than theirs, he could still bleed and die. Auren was probably right. The queen was going to find them sooner or later by way of Saiph, and in the meantime, Orien was *not* going to lose his mate. The light of his soul.

Ice spread out from his hands in a furious whip, spearing through humans quickly, their blood freezing and steaming as soon as it flared. Saiph followed suit, her otherworldly glow filling the darkness as she ripped her glamour away. For a moment Orien could only stare, much like the mortals. He'd never seen a star in all its glory before. He wondered if he would look so graceful if he had lived in the Kingdom of Stars and bathed in starlight all his life?

The glow held the mortals enthralled for a moment before several began to scream. Others tried to cover their eyes, and some began to burn on the spot. Those who could withstand her brightness gazed at Saiph like she was either their saviour or their destruction, and in that moment, he saw her. Valentina. Held between two men whose faces had gone slack at the sight of the star. Orien didn't hesitate. He let his ice run free.

CHAPTER TWENTY-TWO
SAIPH

SAIPH HAD HEARD ORIEN'S FRANTIC CRIES, HAD looked up to see the type of madness only a mate succumbed to when the other was in danger, even if they were mortal. He had needed a distraction, and Saiph was happy to comply. She could only hope the Fates held and her mother would remain in the dark a little while longer.

Saiph secured her glamour back in place, not wanting to tempt fate too much longer, just as Orien's roar split through the sudden silence. He charged on a wave of ice towards two men that Saiph could now see held Valentina and, as though his shout were a signal, the humans charged forward with renewed vigour.

Auren fought in front of Saiph and slightly off to the side, her movements precise and savage as she sliced and stabbed and bled. Saiph had known since last night when Auren had ripped that mortal's heart out with her bare hands that she was capable of savagery—but she hadn't realised how much satisfaction it would give her to see Auren so strong, felling any who crossed her with mere flicks of her wrists.

It didn't seem to matter how many they killed and how many bodies littered the floor. The humans continued to charge forward, and somehow it seemed that there were more of them now than there were before. Soon, even Saiph's arms began to tire, so she knew that Auren and Orien must have truly been struggling.

It was then that it happened.

Saiph didn't even think of the blood debt, or the consequences, just automatically threw one of the remaining daggers strapped to her thigh and saw it land home in the eye of the man with the sword raised above Auren's head.

Auren turned, her eyes wide and face slack with horror, and Saiph felt a wave of sorrow hit her all at once. *What had she done?* Saiph could feel the ties binding her and Auren slipping away, and for a moment there was nothing but tension between them as Auren waited to see Saiph's choice. The blood debt was fulfilled, and Auren was fair game.

Saiph raised her sword and paused as the stars flared brighter, some sort of shift passing through her as an ease that was only associated with one thing relaxed Saiph's shoulders. Home.

Auren seemed to have felt the same shift that Saiph had as the two planes fell back into sync. Saiph knew what her mother would want her to do now that the blood debt was no longer an issue. Kill Auren, torture the information of the heir out of her, and prove her loyalty to her mother yet again.

She is only as powerful as you let her be. They were Auren's words, shockingly similar to Vala's, and for a second, Saiph hesitated. Auren's eyes flickered away from hers, widening in horror.

Saiph turned and saw exactly what had distracted her—the point of a sword that had just run through Orien. For a moment he just swayed, and Saiph heard Valentina screaming as Orien fell to the floor and the crowd fell upon him. No mortal could survive such a wound and regret bit at her. Many more would die like Orien if she did not act. If she did not at least *try*.

Heat prickled the skin of Saiph's cheek, and she turned to find Auren with her hands outstretched.

"Auren, *no*. He's gone—"

Blue, brilliant azure edged in silver burst from Auren's hands and stole Saiph's breath. *A trial by fire*, Saiph had once thought. No true heir to the Kingdom of Stars would burn in starfire, not while they could wield it.

And there she was, body swept up in a tornado of flame, and the humans fell where they stood, screaming until they were no more than dust, heat licking up their bodies and drying out the muddied ground. Valentina ran for safety and the flames did not pursue her. The other mortals weren't so lucky. Auren glanced back at Saiph as she moved through the crowd, something almost like an apology on her face, the tilt of her lips.

Saiph had found her at last.

The heir she had been sent to slay, the queen without a throne—Auren.

Ash clogged Saiph's throat and stung her eyes, but the distant rumble of the clouds sent panic careening through her. There was no way her mother hadn't seen this, not with the way Auren's power called out. It was unimaginable. Her flames burned so hot the air shimmered around her, her skin glowing brown as the gold of her eyes became molten, and Saiph wondered if perhaps the true heir's power rivalled her own.

Lightning struck the ground once, twice, and Saiph recognised it for what it was—command. Her mother bidding for Auren's death from her place beyond the sky.

Auren is a star.

Or at least, half. But blood was blood, and her mother's demand proved Auren's story to be credible. Queen Fallon was likely a kin-killer, and she wanted Saiph to be the same.

Everything inside of her felt like it was screaming. She wanted to rage at the sky, because how could her mother expect this from her? Saiph raised her hands and stopped once more. Her soul was thrashing inside her, and her palms felt slick with sweat. Ragged pants fell from her lips as the last of the humans faded away until only Auren, Valentina, and Orien remained. Orien had the sword out of him and draped on the ground as he shouted his pain, panting as Auren laid her hands to his bloody chest. Valentina knelt by his side and, hesitantly, she offered him her wrist.

Any further doubts Saiph might have had were belied by the sight of the fangs that exploded from Orien's mouth as he bit into the delicate skin Valentina offered up. Lightning thrashed in the sky, growing bolder the longer Saiph remained still. Yet there was no real shock inside her. It felt *right*.

Auren slowly stood and turned to face her. Human faces were beginning to peek outside of the windows of the houses that lined the town square, and still, Saiph stood torn.

"Saiph," Auren said, and the stars seemed to tremble. Her glow brightened, and Auren's shoulders dropped as her fangs slid free.

"You lied to me," Saiph breathed and let her hands fall. Auren seemed relieved but wary. Her hands clenched at her sides, but her face was open, relaxed.

"I had no choice," she replied, gold eyes bright, face speckled with blood, and Saiph felt certain she'd never seen a creature more beautiful.

"You made me look the fool, saving me, hunting with me, letting me f—" Saiph tried to hold onto her anger but found it had been shrouded in desperation, in awe. Something inside her burned so brightly when this strange half-mortal woman was with her. Saiph wasn't sure who she had been before but knew she was somehow *more* when she was with Auren. Realisation clawed at her throat, tightening it to impossible amounts as she looked to the sky.

If she was right about what this feeling meant, then her mother could never know.

Valentina gave a strange cry, and Saiph span, staring in confusion at the barkeep from the tavern as he pressed a blade to Valentina's throat hard enough to let a trickle of red form at her neck.

"This didn't go to plan," he said, and the pain on Valentina's face spoke of betrayal and tugged at a part of Saiph she'd long thought dead or reserved just for Vala. "You would have been fine, Tina, if you'd just stayed out of the way. It was only her they wanted."

Orien's breath rattled but was growing steadier by the moment as the blood rejuvenated him, and he pushed himself up onto his elbows. "You sold us out."

The barkeep sent Orien a look of disgust. "Did you really think we were going to sit back and let you cause a war? Have we not suffered enough? What can she offer us except more blood and death?"

Anger felt like fire as it curled through Saiph's veins, her blood heating and her fangs lengthening.

"You know what task you've been given," he said to Saiph, keeping his hold firm on Valentina to hold Auren and Orien at bay. "I think it's best you complete it now, before your mother decides to punish us all." He nodded to the sky and the brightening of the clouds as starfire began to light them up. To be expending so much power... Saiph shuddered. Her mother must be draining the starlight in the Kingdom of Stars dry.

Instead, Saiph found herself doing something she'd never thought she would do and drew both her swords. A flush spread over Auren's cheeks as she looked at Saiph with something like resignation. Orien had risen from the ground, and Valentina looked torn as he lifted a blade, preparing to strike the barkeep.

"The problem with you mortals," Saiph said as she cocked her head, "is you always seem to think you can give ultimatums." Without hesitating, Saiph lunged impossibly fast across the field and the barkeep's head fell to the ground before he could take his final breath. The clouds flared brighter and Saiph turned to face Auren, knowing full well that this would likely be the last time she would do so. She stalked forward, and Orien threw himself at her. Saiph didn't even look his way as she blasted him back with a wave of her hand. Valentina called out to her, begged her to stop, and Saiph hardened her heart as she stood a breath away from Auren.

Her eyes had cooled, as though the fire that had burned inside her had burnt out, and her bottom lip slid out from between her teeth as Saiph stopped before her. She ran her eyes over Auren's face, taking in the slope of her mouth and the arch of her brow. This woman had lied to her, had tricked and deceived her. Yet, she had given Saiph more freedom than she'd ever had in her life. Cunning, savage, *beautiful*.

"The Fates are cruel," Saiph whispered, letting her

hand brush Auren's cheek, "but I am crueler, *mi anima lux.*"

Auren's face turned pink, and her mouth opened breathlessly but Saiph shook her head.

"You need to go," she announced, and the clouds flashed white with fury, "somewhere where she can't find you." Thunder boomed, and rain began to pour, plastering Saiph's silver hair to her face as she raised both of her swords against the onslaught and fell to her knees. "*Go.*"

Auren shook her head. "I should stay with you, *seren. Victor Victis.* Together."

Saiph kept her gaze solidly fixed on Auren's as she shook her head. "I can't let that happen, and neither can you. Rest assured, if I see you again, we *will* be having words about your many secrets, *stellula.*"

Orien struck, and Saiph turned away as Auren fell to the ground unconscious.

"Get her out of here. I'll buy you as much time as I can."

Orien didn't respond, just heaved Auren over one shoulder and dragged Valentina away by the arm. The faces at the windows were solemn as they watched. They did not run, for who could outrun the stars? Saiph could only hope that Orien could get far enough away before—

Fire burst from the clouds, likely the only warning Saiph was going to get as it struck the ground at her feet. *She wants us to be hers*, Vala had said, and Saiph realised that was the only reason she wasn't yet dead—

control. For it was likely that her mother had never loved her.

"I won't go, Mother. I won't let you kill her. You are *kin-killer* through and through, and one day, she'll be coming for your throne." Saiph let a cocky smile flirt with her mouth as she plunged her swords into the earth and the sky became white once more. She supposed in some ways, the Fates could not have picked her a better mate.

She let out a laugh, imagining her mother's fury as she sat in the sprawling castle atop the city in their kingdom. The sky became ringed with blue, and it was only then that Saiph realised what her punishment was to be—not only her own death, but the destruction of possibly the only semi-functioning town left in the north.

"*Iudi,*" she called and laid her hand against the hilt. "*Vidi,*" she breathed, doing the same to the other. Separately, the swords were powerful, but when combined, Saiph hoped they had the power to defy the stars themselves. She pushed her own magic up, digging down deep into the vestiges of her soul and channelling her fire into the starspun metal, letting them double her strength as she cast it up and out to enclose a bubble over as much of the town as she could manage.

The mortals were crying and cheering in equal parts as the shield raised, thick and gold—like Auren's eyes, Saiph realised with a pang.

Then the sky split open, and starfire raged down in

a crackle of heat that sucked all moisture from the air. If she hadn't already been on her knees she would have collapsed. Her swords burned white hot, and the earth around them crumbled and cracked.

Saiph's body shook as she poured her considerable power into staving off the torrent of blue and white fire that attempted to flood the village. Her mother wasn't just trying to punish... No, she was trying to *raze*.

Her own starfire licked at her skin, and Saiph remembered the mortal rebel she had found on one of her first days on earth, the way she had chosen to burn to death rather than betray her queen. Auren. Saiph now understood the feeling, would have taken this agony a thousand times to spare Auren's life, to give the mortals and stars alike the chance at a better future.

She wished vaguely that she had gotten to kiss Auren a little more, a little longer. Wished her battle with her mother wasn't reduced to this dishonourable attack but instead wished her swords could cleanse that evil from the world personally.

The blue fire was unending, and Saiph swayed through her sweat, digging inside for more power, for more energy, for *more*, and found only the little string of light that connected her to Auren on a soul level. Saiph cradled it, sent an experimental stroke down its length —one last goodbye.

The humans spilled out of their houses, staying far enough away that her heat wouldn't burn them, and

Saiph wanted to smile as they began to sing. It was an old tune, about wars waged and love found and a man who was a star who loved the earth so much he joined with it.

Saiph felt she could empathise. Her magick guttered out, and her swords flared silver in its absence, their magick supporting the remnants of the shield alone now. Her strength gave out, and her face hit the cool mud with a groan. The gold dome above them began to fracture at the same time the fire began to diminish. Had her mother temporarily drained all the starlight from the kingdom for this attack? Saiph would wager she had, but likely wouldn't be around to collect the winnings.

The humans sang louder, bolstered by the hope of impending safety. Some seemed to know who she was and she relaxed as their music became a roar, a mix of her name and the lyrics as their fists hit at the sky. Her shield fell to pieces as everything faded to black.

Saiph smiled one last time. *Nasty little creatures, mortals.*

CHAPTER TWENTY-THREE
AUREN

AUREN WOKE WITH A JOLT AND PUSHED HERSELF UP from the bed she found herself on. What the fuck had happened? The last thing she remembered was Saiph… *Stars*. Saiph had chosen her. Had defied her mother and was now undoubtedly paying the price. Auren rubbed the back of her head with a groan. It had a lump the size of rock on it, and she felt faintly nauseous when she pressed down.

Her heart felt like it would pound straight out of her chest as she cautiously reached for the small thread of light inside her that connected her to Saiph. Blinding pain shot through her spine, and Auren screamed as her skin blistered but remained smooth and her body trembled without ever fighting.

Saiph needed her, and there was only one person who would have taken her away from her mate.

"Orien!" His name seemed to shake the caves as she

screamed, but only Raze appeared, concern heavy in his eyes and tight in his mouth.

"He's not here. He rushed you back through the Forest and then left again," he said before sitting down next to her on the bed. How could it only have been two mere nights since she had been here last? Lying in her bed and fantasising about the way Saiph's mouth had looked when it smirked or the way she glowed and lit up the water in the bathing chamber. Now she was just… Auren gripped the bond tighter, willing her to live. Nothing about her scheme had gone to plan, and she couldn't help but wonder if life would have been better off for her, for Saiph, if she had never followed her that night when the smugglers had taken them.

"Why did he leave?" Auren asked Raze, trying to take her mind off of the pain that wasn't hers.

"He went back for Valentina… and for Saiph."

Hope flared inside her so intensely that she fought for breath, or was that Saiph through the bond, struggling to gasp her last? Was she feeling her fade away with each of Auren's own heartbeats?

Auren leapt up. "I'm going after her."

"You can't—"

"*No*, what I can't do is just sit here and feel her leaving me!"

Raze looked at her steadily. He placed a hand on her shoulder, which she promptly shook off. "She sacrificed herself for *you*. If you leave now, her mother will find you in a heartbeat, and all the people here to boot. Do you think that's what she would have wanted? You in danger? Kara and the others dead?"

Auren shook her head hard as she sank to the dirt floor, bowing her head until her tears made tracks in the dust and every inhalation felt like she was swallowing the earth. A tug flared inside her, a stroke down the bond as if to comfort her, and then a squeeze that made her eyes bulge, and the scream in her throat got stuck.

"No, no, no, no." She didn't even realise she was muttering the words until Raze gripped her shaking form and pulled her into his lap, shushing her gently. Auren ripped at her hair as utter darkness consumed her soul, left with only half of herself after just finding her whole. "I-I think she's gone. Oh stars, Raze, if she's gone... It's my fault, this is all my fault..."

Fire swept through her as her rage tunnelled down, burning nobody but herself. She knew what she had to do, what Saiph's sacrifice had given her the chance for.

"I'm going to kill the queen," Auren whispered to the dark, to Raze, and deep inside Auren, the flickering remnants of her star-bond purred its approval as its light began to grow.

CONTINUE SAIPH & AUREN'S STORY IN
2023 WITH...

THE CLARITY OF
LIGHT

ACKNOWLEDGMENTS

First and foremost – thank you to you, the reader. Your support means everything and I hope you loved reading the first instalment of Saiph and Auren's story.

Sending so much love to my incredible ARC team, I appreciate you guys so much. Thank you for wanting to read my books! I can't wait to share so many more with you all in the future.

Thank you to the brilliant Helena V Paris for your support and feedback – you are the BEST.

This book wouldn't be what it is right now without the help of: Hannah Kaye, my brilliant alpha reader, Katie Wismer, my talented editor, Tamar (niru.sky) for the incredible cover art and Alice Maria Power and Therese (Warickaart) for the incredible interior artwork. Thanks so much to the wider bookish community for your continued support, I don't know what I'd do without you.

Finally, thank you to my partner, Connor, for your endless support.

ABOUT THE AUTHOR

Jade Church is an avid reader and writer of spicy romance. She loves sweet and swoony love interests who aren't scared to smack your ass and bold female leads. Jade currently lives in the U.K. and spends the majority of her time reading and writing books, as well as binge re-watching The Vampire Diaries.

9 781739 896850